PENGUIN BO

Dear Nobody

BERLIE DOHERTY was born in Liverpool in 1943. She
has been writing all her life, with her first work published in the children's pages of her local newspaper
when she wa͏  old. She is the author of
more than s͏  ͏n, teenagers and
adults, and h͏as written plays for ra͏dio, theatre and
television. H͏  slated into more
than twenty͏ and has won many awards,
including the͏ prestigious Carnegie Medal for both
Granny Was͏ a Buffer Girl and *Dear Nobody*. She has
three children͏ and several grandchildren, and lives in
the Derbyshire Peak District.

Berlie Doherty

Dear Nobody

PENGUIN BOOKS

PENGUIN BOOKS

UK | USA | Canada | Ireland | Australia
India | New Zealand | South Africa

Penguin Books is part of the Penguin Random House group of companies
whose addresses can be found at global.penguinrandomhouse.com.

www.penguin.co.uk
www.puffin.co.uk
www.ladybird.co.uk

First published by Hamish Hamilton Ltd 1991
Published in Puffin Books 2001
This edition published 2016
001

Set in 12.2 pt/18 pt Dante MT Std
Typeset by Jouve (UK) Milton Keynes
Printed in Great Britain by Clays Ltd, St Ives plc

A CIP catalogue record for this book is available from the British Library

ISBN: 978–0–141–36894–8

All correspondence to:
Penguin Books
Penguin Random House Children's
80 Strand, London WC2R 0RL

www.greenpenguin.co.uk

Maybe we all want to burn off across the horizon, into space, perhaps, to take off into some unknown territory and meet ourselves out there. This book is a kind of journey, but I don't know yet where it's all going to end.

It all began last January, on a dark evening that was full of sleet. Funny, it's not long ago. I was just a kid then. But today is October 2nd, and this is where I begin to write, where I open a door into the past. It leads into a room in my own house, in a back street not far from the city centre. From the window I can see the lights of thousands of houses that dot out the contours of the hills and valleys of Sheffield. This is my bedroom, full of all kinds of things: my model railway packed in boxes under my bed, my posters and photographs looking like bleak little flags of childhood on the walls. When my wardrobe door swings open it shows just a few T-shirts, a jumper that's too tight, my old trainers. Already it feels like somebody else's room.

I had finished packing my rucksack, ready to take to Newcastle the next day. I took it downstairs and propped it up in the hall. I felt restless; it was too early to go to sleep, but there was nothing left to do to fill in the massive gap between that day and the next: my old life and my future. In a way I was dreading it, leaving all that behind, knowing that nothing would ever be the same again. I hated the thought of saying goodbye. It would be so much easier to just go, just walk through my bedroom door and find myself in a student's room with my posters already on the walls and my guitar by my bed.

At about eight my dad came upstairs with a parcel for me. He stood in the doorway, looking round at the room with its open, empty drawers.

'All packed, Chris?' he said.

Most of all I hated the thought of saying goodbye to Dad.

'Looks as if you'll have to open it all up again. You've got a goodbye present.'

He touched my shoulder lightly as he put the package on my bed. I knew it was going to be hard for him, too. I listened to him as he made his way downstairs, leaning a little on the banister because of a slight limp he has, his hand making that familiar squeaking sound on the wooden rail as he took each step. When I looked down at the parcel I recognized the handwriting on it straight away. It was Helen's. Now I could remember the last time I'd seen her; her face then, the misery I'd felt. I opened up the parcel and shook out the contents over my bed. It was just a pile of letters. I picked them up one by one, not understanding what it was all about. They all began the same way. Dear Nobody. I sat there feeling bleak, with a growing kind of grief in me. Once she and I were the most important people in our world. Is this what I'd become to her? Nobody? I began to read them, in order, trying to make sense of what she was saying in them. They took me back to January. As I said, that's where this journey really begins.

January

Late January. The sort of day that never really starts, when daylight hardly happens and night folds in by mid-afternoon, hushing everything back to sleep again. I was at Helen's house, and we were alone together, lounging back in the big comfortable settee, reading and listening to music, kissing a lot. Helen said she wanted to go upstairs for something and she stood up, trailing her fingers out of my hand, smiling down at me. I didn't want her to go away from me for a second. I followed her up and put some music on in her room, very softly. She has flimsy blue and green silk scarves trailing down the walls; they billow out with the slightest breath of air, as if they were birds drifting. Whether it was the choice of music, or the strange dim light in the room with the curtains still open and these long mothy scarf wings fluttering; or whether it was the way she looked at me, questioning and smiling, when she came to me, I don't know. Maybe it was that something we had never dared talk about had been building up in us for weeks and took us by surprise and storm. It certainly wasn't calculated, that was for sure. Neither of us had known it would happen. But that January evening when the house was empty and a pale and watery moonlight cast the room into white ghostliness, and our favourite music was playing, Helen and I touched each other where we had never touched before and made love.

Afterwards I found it impossible to look at her without smiling. Her mum and dad came back from the shops arguing about which of them had been responsible for forgetting to buy something for that evening's meal, and Robbie came home wet and hungry and was told off for being late. Helen and I sat in the kitchen drinking coffee and touching hands, trying not to look at each other.

'I wonder if they can tell?' I mouthed at her. She looked away from me with a glimmer of laughter in her eyes and stood up to help her mother to unload cleaning powders and unsweetened grapefruit. I watched her stacking things up on the draining board. I could see her reflection in the window, two Helens coming together and separating as she moved backwards and forwards from table to sink, together again, and apart. I wanted her to turn round and smile at me. She knew I was watching her, just as I knew that she was holding me snug in the middle of her thoughts, in spite of all her chattering. It was while I was watching her that I realized that the focus of my life had shifted. For years Dad had been at the centre of everything. Now it was as if he had suddenly turned away in that thinking way he has, his hand just touching his mouth, remembering something that needed to be done, and Helen had stepped smiling into his place.

'I'm starving,' Robbie said. 'What are we having for tea?'

'Nothing,' Mrs Garton said grimly. 'All your father was interested in buying was bottles of Newcastle Brown for his blessed band practice.'

'Bog roll,' said Robbie, emptying a carrier bag. 'Bleach. Window cleaner! I'm famished!'

'Did you write your letter, Helen?' Mr Garton asked suddenly, and Helen flushed and put her hand to her mouth.

'Oh no! I forgot!'

'You forgot!' He raised his voice with disbelief. 'You forgot!'

'What's she forgotten now?' Mrs Garton demanded.

'Only the most important thing in her life,' Mr Garton told her. 'Her acceptance. How on earth could you have forgotten, Helen?'

Helen looked at me quickly, a tiny glance of accusation, and away again. 'I'll do it now,' she said. 'There's still time.'

'What's the matter?' I asked. All I knew was that Helen had upset her dad, that he was visibly shocked and disappointed in her, and that for some reason it was my fault.

'Nothing at all,' Mr Garton said, tight in his throat. 'The girl gets a full offer from the Royal Northern College of Music to do Composition and she forgets to write back and accept it. That's all.'

'I'll do it now, I said,' Helen told him. She was nearly crying. 'I've got till tomorrow, Dad.'

'I'd better go,' I said.

'I think you had,' said her mother, arms folded, looking from one to the other of us.

Helen came to the door with me.

'I'm sorry, Helen,' I whispered.

'It's okay,' she said. 'It's just that it means so much to Dad. Nearly as much as it means to me.'

I put my arms round her. It meant that in October our ways would separate, mine to Newcastle, hers to Manchester. But October was a long way away.

'It's raining,' she said. 'Do you want a brolly? I could lend you the yellow one Nan gave me for Christmas. In fact, you can keep it. It makes me look like a daffodil.'

'No. I love the rain.' I had to keep clearing my throat. 'I love you, Nell.'

'Helen, shut that door! It's like a fridge in here!' her mother called.

Helen pushed me off the doorstep and pulled the door to behind her. She put her arms up and looped them round my neck. I could smell her hair.

'I want it to happen all over again,' I said. 'Now.'

'You'd better go.'

'I don't want to.'

'We could stand out here in the rain all night,' she suggested. 'But my hair would frizz up and you'd go off me.'

'I know when I'm beaten. I'll ring you.'

I ran off, dancing backwards, as Helen raised her hand for a moment with the light of the open door behind her, framing her. It was like a pose for a photograph. I keep remembering it. Then she closed the door. It was full dark by then. The rain had sleet in it and slanted across the street lamps like long glass splinters, separate and sharp. I unzipped my jacket and ran with it flapping loose and with my face tilted up and my mouth open. I had a sudden wild thought that I would like to run across the road into the park and stand naked in the sleet. I would keep on running as naked as a fish through Endcliffe Park and on up past Wiremill Dam and Forge Dam, and past the swings and slides where I used to play when I was little, and on and on till I was right up on the dark moors.

'I'll take Helen up there,' I thought. 'When it snows. I'll

take Helen up there and we'll lie down in the deep deep snow and keep each other warm.'

A car pulled up beside me, whooshing spray against my legs. The driver beeped and I looked round, zipping up my jacket, cursing. She beeped again and leaned over to open the passenger door.

'Get in,' she said. 'You're soaked to the skin.'

I climbed in, glad now to be somewhere dry. 'I'm not supposed to accept lifts from strange women.'

'I'd be hard up if I was thinking of abducting a skinny rat like you, Chris.' She looked in her mirror and edged out into the traffic again. It was the rush hour. Sleet fizzed against the windscreen, fracturing the dazzle of lights.

'You mustn't go out of your way,' I told her.

'I wouldn't dream of it. I've got some manure in the boot to deliver to your dad. You can carry it home instead, if you like. It would save my petrol.'

I leaned my head back on the rest and closed my eyes. I had a sudden absurd desire to start singing. I would have loved to have told her about Helen.

'I think I should call you Jill now,' I said.

'I wish you would. I've always hated the "aunty" bit. I always feel as if an aunty should be knitting you nice jumpers and asking you round to tea.'

'I'm a deprived nephew, then. I knew there was

something wrong with my life.' I gave a long, satisfied yawn. 'I'm tired,' I murmured. My head was in a wonderful foggy sleepy spin. 'Really tired.' I closed my eyes.

I rang Helen as soon as I had a chance to. I just wanted to hear her voice. I stood in the hall grinning and not saying anything and I could tell that Helen at the other end was smiling into the receiver.

'What're you doing?' I asked.

'Smiling.'

'I knew you were.'

'What're you doing?'

'Smiling back.'

'Helen. I need the phone.' That was her mother. She does it every time.

'I'll have to go, Chris. See you tomorrow?'

'We've got a trip to Rotherham.'

'Rotherham! Our school's going to Geneva at Easter.'

'We're going to see *Much Ado* at the Civic.'

'Helen!'

'Okay, Mum. See you, Chris.'

I stood listening to the buzz of the dead phone, imagining her going back up those mossy green stairs of theirs to her room, pulling the curtains closed, stopping perhaps to look out at the sleet against the street lamps.

'You're sweet. You're so lovely,' I murmured as I put the receiver down.

'Thanks,' my dad said, coming down the stairs behind me. 'I didn't think you'd noticed. How about doing the washing-up, Chris?'

I joined my brother in the kitchen. Guy had filled up the sink with bubbles, and as soon as I went in he started flicking them at me. He always does it.

'Give over,' I said, flicking back. I scooped up a handful of froth and eased it on to Guy's head when he turned away to get a tea towel.

'You can do the pans,' Guy said. 'They're all burnt, and it serves you right for gassing on the phone for hours.'

He kept walking round the kitchen with that lacy pyramid on his head, his glasses still flashing earnest intelligence. I don't know how he does it.

'Dad,' I shouted. 'Did you know the snow's coming into the kitchen!'

'Very pretty,' said Dad, glancing in on his way past. 'Love the headdress, Guy.'

Guy walked past him, the tea towel flung across his shoulder, and caught sight of his reflection in the mirror. He made a ball of the tea towel with his fist and hurled it at me and I charged at him with another handful of froth and stuffed it down his neck. We were yelling our heads off. He's all knees and elbows and chins. It's like fighting with a sackful of coat hangers. The cat dived for the cat flap, backed in again when it saw the sleet, and darted upstairs.

'Will you two stop it!' Dad shouted. 'I'd rather have a pair of two-year-olds in the house any day.'

Guy cupped another handful of froth against my chin, where it dangled like a threadbare beard.

'Very funny, Guy.' I kept it there, letting it wobble as I talked. We were both gasping for breath. I love fighting with Guy. 'But I'm above such childishness.'

'Since when?' asked Guy.

I tapped the side of my nose. 'That's my business,' I said. I wish I could wink. I have to close both eyes. Guy winked for me, understanding nothing, and I leapt on him again.

'Pans,' shouted Dad from the front room. 'Homework!'

I let Guy go and he hopped upstairs to do his essay. I gave the pans a good beating, too. I could hear Guy's cassettes thumping away upstairs. He has terrible taste in music. I'll have to educate him. I finished off the pans, leaving the worst one to soak even though it had been soaking for three days already since my disastrous bean curry had turned into carcinogen. Helen would be sitting in her room doing her maths project by now, her books spread round her, her chin propped in her hand.

I sat with Dad for a bit, watching the nine o'clock news. The room smelt slightly of manure because Jill and I had had to carry the bags through to the yard. All through tea I'd wanted to talk to Dad about something, and now that we were alone together at last I didn't know where to start.

'It's all politics these days,' I said.

'You want to take it in,' Dad said. He had a way of pouting out his lower lip and stroking it with his fingertips when the news was on. Guy said that was why he could never bear to watch the news. 'It's bound to come up on your General paper, you know. This is history.'

I groaned.

'And it's happening now. That's what history is, Chris.'

'Give over, Dad. We're getting it all the time at school, too.'

'I should hope so. It's the only thing that matters, you know, what happens to people. You can keep your pop shows.'

'I'm going up,' I said.

'At this time?'

'I'm shattered.' I hadn't asked him, and I was disappointed

in myself. It's hard to say the things that matter, but I don't know why.

'I'll have to get you a dishwasher,' Dad murmured.

I wrote a song for Helen. I worked out some chords for it on my guitar, then tried it all again in a minor key. I wrote another verse and practised singing it, standing with one foot on the bed so I could balance my guitar on my knee. The last verse was so good that I sang it again, much louder this time. Guy threw a book against the joining wall, and the cat fled downstairs again and headbutted the cat flap. I wrote the chords down so I wouldn't forget them and then put a blank cassette into my radio-recorder and sang it all through, strumming softly, picking out a few bass runs with my thumb. I thought I might rerecord it the next day so I could do it all finger-style, but I needed to get a new plectrum. The one I was using was the plastic tie-tag from a sliced loaf and it had split. I tried it in another key. Helen had taught me all the chords I knew on the guitar. One day I wanted to just wake up and be able to play like Jimi Hendrix. I decided I would post the cassette as it was through Helen's letter box on my way to school next day.

It was nearly midnight by then. I went back downstairs. Dad was sitting with his feet up on the settee watching a late film.

'You shouldn't be watching this,' I told him. 'It's rude.'

'I close my eyes when the naughty bits come on.'

'Dad,' I said. 'What happened to you and Mum?' I'd had no idea I was going to say that just then.

The woman on the television screen smiled knowingly and murmured to me. I thought Dad hadn't heard me at first, the way I'd blurted it out. If he'd asked me to repeat it I wouldn't have been able to.

'You know what happened.' He seemed to be waiting for the woman to speak again. 'She walked out.'

'I mean, why?'

Dad looked at me sharply as if he was going to tell me to mind my own business. I wouldn't have blamed him. Then he pulled a face. He swivelled himself round on the settee into a sitting position as if it was all a great effort, as if he was an old man stiff with lumbago these days.

'She met a feller, didn't she, and he was younger than me with a bit more hair on top and he wore natty jumpers and he read a lot of books. And she decided she liked him better than me and off she went.'

We watched the screen for a bit. The woman had a thin face like a snake. She flickered her tongue when she laughed.

'She just went, just like that,' Dad went on quietly. 'Went off. I came home one night and I'd done a shift, I was dead tired, you know, and there she was standing in the hall with her coat on and this feller was with her.' He bent down and put one of his shoes on. 'Tying his shoe laces or something, hiding his face, that's what he was doing. And she told me she was leaving.'

'Did you know him?'

Dad blew out his lips. 'As a matter of fact, I did. Not well, of course. But he'd been round a couple of times.'

We both stared at the television. I didn't dare look at my dad. It was as if, now he'd started, he couldn't stop. It was as if he was talking to himself almost. Out of the corner of my eye I could see him stroking his lip. I daren't move. The television voices murmured on.

'Didn't suspect a thing. That's what your mother hated most about me, of course. She said I'd got no imagination.' He laughed briefly, a sharp bark of a laugh. The couple in the play were rowing now. A close-up of the woman showed that she was crying.

'Are those tears real?' Dad said. 'I bet they use some kind of oil or something. Her make-up's not running, and she'd have to be wearing some with all those lights.'

'She's not wearing much else.' I could feel my voice breaking into a nervous giggle.

'Funny,' Dad said. 'I didn't know how much I loved your mother till she told me she was leaving me. You'd think

I would have hated her. I did later. No one likes to be rejected, you know. I hated her because she didn't want me. And I hated her because she was splitting up a family. I didn't want that to happen, and I was powerless to stop it. How old were you then?'

'Ten. Guy was six.'

'You see. Guy cried for his mum every night. How could I explain to the kid? And you . . . "where's Mum, where's Mum" . . . every five minutes. How could I explain to you that she wasn't coming back? So it helped, being able to hate her. But I'll tell you something else, Chris, and this'll shock you a bit. I used to wish that she was dead.'

The drama on the screen was suddenly interrupted by noisy adverts. A smiling troupe of mushrooms danced its way across a table and dive-bombed into a bowl of soup.

My dad leaned forward in his chair, intent on the mushrooms. He was fiddling about with his watchstrap as if it was suddenly too tight for him, twisting it and twisting it on his wrist, tugging hairs with it. 'If she'd died, you see, I could have got it over with. There's ways of dealing with death. There's funerals and flowers and crying. It would have been terrible, but I would have known absolutely certainly that she wasn't going to come back and that I was never, never going to see her again and somehow I'd have got on with my life and with you kids. But while ever someone's alive there's always a chance that they'll come back again, so you never quite let go. I wanted her back, however much I hated her for going.'

I felt my throat tightening. I wished Dad would stop now. I wished he'd stop talking. I wished I could switch off the television but I daren't. I was afraid of the silence and of having to look at him again and talk normally. I sat with my head back and my eyes closed tight. Even then I could see the dance of light from the flickering screen: flash, and flash, and flash. Dad's voice was a dull monotone.

'I used to think of her enjoying herself with this natty bloke with all his books. And I knew that she couldn't be happy. Not really. I knew she'd be going through hell. Don't tell me any woman can walk away from her own kids and carry on as if nothing had happened. I think she went through hell.'

There was some fancy guitar music on the screen. The man and woman were walking hand in hand along a beach. I thought it might be Brighton.

'You think you're the only one in the world it's happened to till you go down the pub and talk about it. Makes you wonder. What's it all about? Love? I don't know what love is. It's a con trick to keep the human race going, that's all it is.'

'Why didn't you get married again or something?'

'Ouch!' Dad shook his hand as if his fingers had been burnt. He switched off the television abruptly as the snaky woman pouted out her lips for another kiss, and went into the kitchen. I could hear him filling the kettle.

'Ovaltine, Chris?'

I sauntered into the kitchen. I leaned on the door jamb casually, my hands deep in my pockets.

'I just wondered, Dad. You don't happen to have Mum's address, do you?'

Dad lifted two mugs from the cupboard. He'd made them himself, down in the cellar. One day he planned to give up work and make a living 'pottering about' as he called it. As he spooned Ovaltine powder into them he spilled some and carefully wiped it up, and wiped the whole surface and the kettle before he answered me. 'I should have. Somewhere.'

I passed him a bottle of milk from the fridge. The cat strolled over to him and eyed him patiently.

'Why?' Dad asked. He eased the cat out of the way with his foot and returned the milk to the fridge.

'I was thinking I might go and see her some time.' I kept my voice light and casual. ''Night, Dad.' I took my cup and went upstairs slowly, sipping at it while I walked. I couldn't even begin to explain why I wanted to see my mother after all those years, except that maybe it was something to do with Helen. I would have liked my mother to meet her, I suppose.

I listened to the tape again. My head was full of Helen now; brimming with her. I lay in bed and couldn't sleep for thinking of her. A new verse for the song started buzzing in my head, and I decided to go downstairs and have some toast and marmalade and write it down.

And there was Dad, still sitting in the front room with a cup of cold Ovaltine in his hands, just staring at the way the sleet pattered and slid against the window panes.

February

I don't think I would have dared to ask those questions about my mother if it hadn't been for what had happened between Helen and me. I felt as if I was peering through a door into another room in my life. I wanted to know now what kind of a person my mother was; even if it hurt, I wanted to know. Once upon a time she and my father had loved each other, when he was a young man and she was a girl. I knew that this house that we lived in was the house he had been born in, and that he had looked after his parents here till they died. What must it have been like for my mother, coming here as a new wife? I knew she was younger than him. Had the house been full of ghosts for her? Old furniture, faded carpets, brown photographs; Grandad's carver chair; Grandma's tea set; the polished wooden cutlery canteen; the chiming clock. I never knew my grandparents, but their presence is here, all right. But when I tried to imagine my mother here, it was as if I was holding up a candle inside a darkened room and noticing things for the first time because they looked so different now. There were no ghosts of my mother in the house. None at all.

It had taken me days to write the letter to her. Helen had helped me, and then we had started it again and rewritten it several times.

'Are you sure you're doing the right thing?' Helen asked me. 'You won't bring her back, you know. Not after all this time.'

But I didn't want to bring her back. I wanted to meet her again, that was all. I think I just wanted to believe in her, if you know what I mean. The mother in my memories was someone who read stories to me at night and held my hand to cross the road. She didn't fit in anywhere now. It was as if she wasn't real any more.

I carried the letter round in my pocket for a few days and in the end Helen posted it for me. After a couple of weeks I stopped looking out for a reply. I was nothing to my mother, after all. I was a speck of dust, and I had blown away. But when her letter came after nearly a month all I could think about was showing it to Helen. We were going out together that evening, out to the moors in the dark, and then for a drink. My letter was a warm secret in my pocket, waiting to be shared.

It was the night of the total eclipse of the moon, which had been promised for 6.52. It was all a great disappointment, the whole thing. The sky was completely covered in cloud that night, it was drizzling, and Helen was in a rotten mood.

We had taken a bus out to Fox House so we could see the eclipse away from the orange glare of the city lights. We walked up the track towards the moors, below Stanage Edge. In the darkness sheep rustled through the sodden ferns.

'I can't tell which direction we're supposed to be looking in, even,' moaned Helen.

'Try up.' I put my arm round her. 'A quarter of a million miles up.' She tensed away from me. It's not like her to be moody.

'I'm cold and I'm fed up and I've missed my tea for this.'

'It's supposed to look like a ball of blood,' I told her. 'That would be something to see, wouldn't it?'

'Yuk,' she said, and started to walk down the track, which was so rough and stony that she kept losing her footing. I could hear her grumbling away to herself. 'Are you staying out here all night?' she called.

I caught up with her and held her hand in my pocket, snug as a glove. 'Imagine seeing the dawn from up here! Why don't we do that one night?' I felt warm at the thought of it. She was scuttling along with her head down and I stepped right in front of her so she had to stop close up to me. 'We could bring a tent, Helen, and we could watch the sun go down, and see the moon and stars coming out. And the next day we'd watch the dawn . . . Imagine watching it spreading pink and golden across the sky . . .'

'And then we'd stagger into school for registration and tell my mum that we'd missed the last bus home.'

'We could come in June. We could just sleep out in the heather – we wouldn't need a tent, then. There'd just be us . . .'

'And a few sheep nibbling at us.'

'We could come on the longest day. There's a cave along the edge – we could sleep in there.'

'Meanwhile, let's go home and have some beans.' Helen pushed past me. 'I'm famished, Chris. Actually, I feel sick, I'm so hungry.'

When we were on the bus I showed her the letter. I'd been waiting for the right moment to share it with her, but I gave up on that. I kept looking at her, waiting for her to show some of the excitement I'd felt when I found the letter on the hall floor that morning. I'd known who it was from even before I looked at the postmark. I think I even recognized her writing, which is the sort that looks really artistic from a distance and is just a scrawl of shapes when you get close to. It had arrived just as I was setting off for school, and I'd pushed it into my pocket quickly before my dad saw it. I didn't want him to be hurt, whatever happened. I had read it at school during form period and, predictably, my mate Tom had seen me reading it and had snatched it off me. He's so infantile at times.

'Chris's got a love-letter,' Tom had said, waving it in the air.

'Get lost,' I told him. He was trying to taunt me into having a scrap with him for it, but then I think he must have recognized something in the way I looked at him. I really hated him at that moment. I wasn't laughing.

'Hand it over, Wilson.'

'Can't read it, anyway.' He just dropped it on the floor for me to pick up. It was a bit screwed up by then. So was I, to tell the truth. During the day I kept stealing furtive glances at it. She really does have terrible handwriting. I'd had to guess at most of the words. I tried to put a picture of my mother in my head, and couldn't. I remembered a blue coat with little velvet buttons, and how it smelt of cold air when she came in at night.

'Want to see this?' I asked Helen on the bus. I handed it casually to her as if it didn't matter really whether she did or not, and waited for her expression to change. She peered at the letter and handed it back to me.

'Is she a doctor or something? I can't read a word of it.'

'It says, *"Dear Christopher".*'

'Christopher! That's a bit formal.'

My voice was shaking a little as I read on. I cleared my throat and took a breath. ' *"Thank you for your letter. It was a great surprise,"* I think it says. *"I'm sorry I didn't reply straight away but I've only just returned from the Alps. I don't know if you know but I'm a professional photographer. I've been working on a commission to illustrate a mountaineering book. I climb too, of course, with Don."* ' I put the letter down for a moment. My breath seemed to have left me. I blew out my lips and carried on. ' *"This has been a wonderful job for me, and is going to take up several more months, I should think. Yes, do come and see me. It would be lovely. With best wishes, Joan."* '

'Joan!'

'What else could she have put? With love from Mummy?'

I gazed down at the letter again. I'd been looking forward to sharing it with Helen. All day I'd imagined showing it to her.

'What d'you think?' I asked her.

'I don't like her.' Helen took the letter from me again. She really was in a mood.

'You've never even met her.'

'I don't like the way she calls you Christopher, for a

start. What's wrong with Chris? Christopher's so formal, as if she's never met you in her life. And then she goes and calls herself "Joan" at the end.'

'I thought that was brilliant. It's a way of saying, our relationship is different now, let's be friends.'

'Great!' said Helen. 'I'll just disappear for eight years while you're an annoying brat and let's be friends now you've grown up.'

I stared out of the window. I could feel my neck burning red. 'Anything else you don't like about her, while you're at it?'

'I don't like the way she goes on and on about being a photographer and a climber and having commissions and all that.'

'She doesn't go on and on.'

'She sounds like a show-off. She hasn't said a thing about you. How're your A levels? How's your dad? How's Guy? Have you still got the cat? All she's interested in is herself.'

I took the letter back and folded it up slowly. I sat with it still in my hands, staring out at my own reflection and, beyond that, into the darkness.

' "My dear Lady Disdain",' I muttered.

'She makes a point of saying she hasn't got time to see you.'

'All right. All right.'

28

'You asked me. I'm only telling you because you asked me.'

'I wish I hadn't shown it to you now.'

Helen touched my hand. 'I don't think you should try to see her, Chris. You'll get hurt. I've thought that all along.'

'That's my business, isn't it?' The bus swung suddenly into the glare of house lights. I stood up. 'I'll come back with you.'

'You don't have to.'

'I'll come back with you.'

We walked along in silence, holding hands. I felt angry and upset, as if we were on the verge of a row. I wish I knew what was going on in her head. I can't fathom her sometimes. That's what's exciting about her, but she's never like this usually. It was as if all the warmth had gone out of her. We'd had our first row last month, and even that hadn't been like this. The first row had been my fault, I admit it. It had started when we had bumped into her best friend, Ruthlyn, and as she passed us she had said in a loud whisper, 'Behave yourselves this time!'

'What's she on about?' I had asked. Ruthlyn's the sort of girl who loves to embarrass people.

'What d'you think?' Helen had teased.

'You never told her!'

'Of course I did.'

I couldn't believe that, you see. I felt betrayed. 'Not everything?'

'She's my best friend,' Helen had said, as if that explained everything.

'What's that got to do with us?'

'I bet you told your mates. All boys brag about what they do with their girlfriends.'

I'd bragged often enough about nearly doing it. As a matter of fact I'd often casually given the impression that I'd done far more than I actually had done. But I couldn't have told anyone about that special night. I imagined Tom bawling it round the classroom at school. I imagined the words he'd have used about us, reducing us both, cheapening it. There's no way I could have told him. It was too important to share.

'Well. You're wrong. You should know me better,' I said. 'But I never thought you'd go around telling everyone.'

'I didn't say I'd told everyone. I said I'd told my best friend.'

I'd chewed away at all this like a dog picking at the scraps of meat on a bone, shaking it and gnawing it till it was dry and tasteless.

'I suppose you've told your mother as well,' I'd said. We were walking apart, our hands thrust in our pockets, not looking at each other. All I wanted to do was to hold her, and I didn't know how.

'As a matter of fact I haven't. She's not that sort of mother. I wish she was. You know how awkward she is, Chris. Ruthlyn tells her mother everything.'

'So I suppose she knows now, too.'

'I shouldn't think so. Of course she wouldn't. There's no need for her mother to know about you and me. Chris . . .' Helen had stopped and put her hand on my arm. It was like a spark of electricity. 'Please don't be mad at me.'

'I can be what I like.' Actually, now the danger was passed, I realized I was beginning to enjoy my anger a little bit. I wasn't quite ready to give in.

'You don't own me, you know, just because of what we did together,' Helen had said then, so quietly that I could hardly hear her. 'You have no rights over me at all.' And it was that quietness that had been like the touch of icy hands on me, as if she was so much older than me and knew so much more than me. I felt as if I could slip away from her, as easy as anything, and that she would let me.

And now it looked as if it was all happening again, as if we were walking on cracked ice that threatened to spin us away from each other.

'What's up with you these days?' I asked her.

'Nothing.'

'I seem to be upsetting you for some reason.'

'Nobody's upsetting me. Just go home or something, Chris. Don't keep on at me.'

I shrugged and kept on walking, holding my head up, whistling slightly as if I didn't care.

'It's not you, Chris. I started the day wrong. I shouldn't have come out, but we said tonight, so I came.'

I wanted to comfort her, and to be comforted by her. I wish we could have started the evening again. I glanced at her and she looked away. Her face was cast bronze in the light of the street lamps, and her eyes were gleaming. We had come to her road, big houses set in their own gardens, all the windows lit, the curtains closed to. I thought of all the families carrying on their particular lives, all the houses in the world, people loving each other and hurting each other, people closing curtains round themselves.

When we came to her house she left her door open and I followed her in. The house smelt of paint. Helen slipped her shoes off and I remembered to wipe mine on the door mat. I never do that in our house.

Ted Garton, her dad, was singing loudly to himself in the kitchen. He reduced it to a self-conscious hum when we went in, as if he was practising a new tune.

'How's the guitar coming on, Chris?' He always says that. He never really knows what to say to me. It's a good job I play guitar.

'Not bad. Wish it was an electric, though.'

'When are you going to join my band, eh?'

'Can't do jazz chords. They're too hard.'

I was watching Helen as she stood by the window, lifting her hair and letting it fall again on her shoulders. I could see her reflected in the glass. She's miles away, I thought. Where are you, Nell?

Mr Garton grunted and sat down, smiling at us both, ready to let us chat to him. We didn't talk. Helen still stood by the window lifting and lifting her hair, and I couldn't take my eyes off her. I thought my staring at her must make her turn round to me again. I felt helpless. Ted Garton cleared his throat a few times and at last seemed to realize that he was in the way. After a bit he hummed loudly again and went into the back room and began to play the piano. Soon he would be so absorbed in his playing that he wouldn't hear his wife Alice if she came in to complain, and the members of his band would have to be let in by whoever else was in the house because he'd never hear the doorbell.

'Talk to me, Helen,' I said. I went over to her and turned her round, tilting up her chin so I could look at her. She clamped shut her eyes and set her mouth in a firm, hurt line. I wanted to kiss away the hurt, whatever it was, but she just bowed her head down again, and her mother came in. In the brief look that I caught before I let go of her I saw that she was afraid.

Helen's mother had flecks of white paint on her hair and her nose, her glasses and her hands. She was wearing an old shirt of her husband's. She sank down into a kitchen chair and slipped off her shoes. One of her stockings had a toe hole in it, and she curled her big toe under to hide it.

'I'm tired out,' she said. 'Put the kettle on, Helen.'

'I'll do it,' I said. Helen stayed where she was, staring out into the night. I had to squeeze past her to get to the sink.

'If you think there's a dinner waiting for you in the oven, you're mistaken, my girl,' said Mrs Garton. 'It was help yourself night tonight. I've been busy.'

'I don't want any,' said Helen.

'I'll do you some beans if you like,' I offered.

She shrugged. 'I'm not hungry.'

She sat down opposite her mother, and began systematically shredding the corners of a straw table mat till her mother leaned across and snatched it from her.

I put two cups of coffee on the table and went back to the drainer for my own. Helen pushed hers away from her.

'And what's wrong with that?' her mother demanded.

'I don't want it,' said Helen. 'I don't like coffee.'

'First I've heard!' I laughed, surprised. 'You drink it by the gallon!'

'I didn't ask for it in the first place.'

'Take it through to your father, then,' said Mrs Garton. 'It'll wake him up out of his trance, maybe, before that gang of his arrives.'

Helen sighed and did as she was told. Mrs Garton eyed me over the rim of her cup. I felt uncomfortable. It was as if she was trying to probe into my mind. I always felt awkward when I was left on my own with her.

'Had a tiff?'

'Not as far as I know.'

'Looks to me as if you have, whether you know it or not,' she said. 'I'm always having tiffs with Ted, and he never seems to notice either.' She yawned. 'Men! Insensitive bunch, the lot of you.' She swivelled round to look at Helen as she came back in. 'I think you're sickening for something,' she said. 'Your eyes are watery. You might be in for a dose of flu.'

'I think I might be,' Helen agreed. 'I think I might have an early night.'

'You do,' said Mrs Garton, satisfied. She nodded at me. 'Looks as if you've got your marching orders, young man.'

I shifted uncomfortably on my high stool. 'I'll just finish my coffee first.' They were ganging up on me.

She went over to the sink and squirted washing-up liquid on to her hands. She scrubbed at them viciously with a green scratchy cloth. 'You heard the girl,' she said, her back to us both, hunched and vigorous over the sink. 'She's tired. It's all this schoolwork. You can't have a social life and study for A levels. I know that. You shouldn't go dragging her out in the rain like this. She could have watched that eclipse of the moon on the news, for goodness' sake. You take up too much of her time, Chris. She's got enough on with her schoolwork.'

I looked anxiously at Helen, but she wasn't giving me any help. She seemed to have slipped back into her daydreaming. The cracks in the ice had deepened, and she was floating away from me fast, fast, over black water. 'Right,' I said at last. Everything was wrong with me all of a sudden. My hands had grown too big to stuff in my pockets, even. 'I think I'll be off, then.'

Helen followed me into the hall. The door to the kitchen was still open, and I could just see Mrs Garton leaning back slightly in her chair, as though she was straining to hear us above the sound of her husband's piano playing. I felt desperate, as if I was seeing Helen for the last time. 'Come outside a minute,' I said.

We closed the door slightly. Helen put her arms up to

loop my neck and put her head against my chest. My heart was lurching like a bird.

'What's wrong?' I whispered.

'Nothing. Nothing, honestly.'

'You've been so strange. I feel terrible. I thought you were going off me.'

She let out her breath. I stroked her hair, a little comforted by the warmth of her against me.

'You'd tell me, wouldn't you, if you were going off me? If there was somebody else?' My lips were sticking together with nervousness.

'There's nobody else. Don't be daft, Chris.' Her voice was so low that I could hardly hear her.

'Then what is it?'

A car pulled up in the drive and two men got out, slamming the doors noisily. They were both carrying instrument cases.

'I can't tell you,' she whispered.

'Aye aye, it's a kiss and a cuddle, is it?' said one of them, a big bearded man in his late forties. His beer belly squashed up against us as he squeezed past. 'Love's young dream. Takes me back a bit, that does.'

She was soft and warm in my arms again.

'Don't let us disturb you! Just carry on!' said the other man, winking at me.

'We won't,' I murmured. I was wishing them miles away.

'I might be in for a touch of flu, like Mum said.' Helen pulled away from me. 'I'll stay off school tomorrow.'

'I'll come round,' I said.

Another band member roared up on his motorbike.

'Don't,' said Helen. 'Meet me after school on Wednesday.'

'That's years away,' I said, fool for her that I was. 'I can't wait that long.'

I urgently wanted to say things that no one else should hear but her mother was coming up the hall, her paint shirt draped over her shoulder. She leaned against the doorway, arms folded, watching the motorbike man. He propped his bike up on its stand and took a pair of drumsticks out of the pannier.

'How d'you fit your drum kit into that?' she asked.

'My car's packed in,' he told her. 'I'll be banging pans tonight, Alice.'

'That'll please the neighbours, anyway.' Alice laughed and held open the door for him. She tapped Helen on the shoulder. 'Thought you were having an early night, Madam,' she said.

'Wednesday, then,' I said. Helen squeezed my hand and followed her mother and the little drummer back into the house. But I stood for ages watching the closed door, and the curtains being pulled across the window where the men were practising, and the light going on upstairs in the room where Helen slept. She didn't look at me once, I thought. I've been out with her for four whole hours and she hasn't looked me in the face once. What is it, Nell?

When I got home my dad was in the cellar. He came up, wiping his hands on his boiler suit. He was carrying a mug that he'd made. 'Don't you think this is a lovely design, Chris?' he asked.

I hardly looked at it. 'Marvellous,' I said.

My dad looked disappointed. 'It's not that bad. What's bugging you?'

'Nothing.' I dug my hands in my pockets and found my mother's letter there, as cold and shocking now to my touch as a handful of melting ice cubes. 'I've got an essay to do for tomorrow.' I ran upstairs and sat on my bed to reread the letter. Helen was right. My mother had taken four weeks to answer and hadn't even asked me how I was. She hadn't bothered to make contact with me for eight years; birthday and Christmas presents had come as money paid into my father's bank account. She'd made a point of telling me how busy she was, how full and successful her life was, how much she had in common with her natty bloke, as if I cared. I wished I hadn't written to her. She didn't need me, that was quite obvious. What a fool I would have felt if I had decided to go to her house. What on earth would we have said to each other?

'Hello, Mum. Hello, Joan, I mean. I'm Christopher.' I tried it out loud. I tried to sound casual and pleased. I tried to sound like Tom, deepening my voice. I did a falsetto bit for my mother. ' "My, you've grown. Look, Christopher, these are my new crampons. This is my zoom lens." "They're nice, Joan." "This is Don." "Hello, Don. Hi, Don. How d'you do? You've got a lot of hair on top! What a lot of books, Don!" '

I screwed up the letter and chucked it in the waste paper basket. Well, if she didn't need me, I didn't need her.

I kept trying to ring Helen. She never seemed to be around. Her mother always said, 'She's working, Chris,' as if she was trying to make me feel guilty for disturbing her. She does work hard, though. Both her parents have always seen to that. I think they have ambitions for her; I think she has for herself, too. I wondered what my mother expected me to do with my life. I don't suppose she even thought about it.

The next few days brought gales, worse than any I could remember. When we were watching television the carpet kept lifting up in the middle as if it was riding on the waves of the sea. The cat watched its breathing centre, tail twitching, back arched to pounce. During the night we had to drag Guy's mattress into my room because his bedroom window came bursting away from its hinges, even though we'd tried sticking it down with Sellotape and Blu-tack. I quite enjoyed having Guy in my room again. We sat up in bed till all hours talking. Guy was excited about the gales.

'You know what's brought this lot on, don't you?' he said. 'It's the greenhouse effect. We can conquer space and invent computer chips and now we're affecting the climate too! We're proving how powerful we are.'

'Don't talk rot, brat,' I told him. 'You don't know anything. We're proving how powerless we are. Our planet is set on self-destruct, and we haven't got the power to stop it happening. Everything's controlled by fate. It's all been planned.'

'Like a computer program?'

We settled down for sleep, listening to the wind moaning like a lurking beast round the houses in the street. During the night the top of our chimney toppled off and crashed down the roof tiles and on to the road. I woke up sweating. I realized that I'd been dreaming about Helen and that when the crash had come she had just rolled away from me and broken into little pieces of bone, and I'd run after her and crouched down to pick up all the splinters in my hands. All I'd had to wrap them in was a blue coat with velvet buttons.

I rang her up before I left for school. The dream was still haunting me like the images of a film.

'Are you all right?'

There was a long pause at the other end.

'Are you?' I asked, scared.

'I don't know.'

'What d'you mean? What's the matter?'

'Meet me after school. I'll have to go. Mum's in a right mood with me.'

She put the receiver down quickly and I ran out, late. My heels scrunched the pieces of chimney pot on the pavement. I booted them into the gutter and ran on, head into the wind. Helen wanted to see me again. That was all that mattered.

Her school was a couple of miles away from mine, and it was uphill all the way. I sprinted there. By the time I came to the railings there was no breath left in me. I leaned against the wall, panting, till my breathing was back to normal. There was no sign of Helen. There was hardly anyone around by now, but I guessed she would be waiting for me in the sixth-form centre, out of the wind. I felt self-conscious, walking up the drive of someone else's school.

I'd been there for football matches when I was younger, and soon after I'd started going out with Helen I'd come to watch her in a concert. Actually, it was when I was watching her in the show that I'd realized that she was different from any other girl I'd ever known. I expected to feel embarrassed, watching her dancing on the stage in front of everyone, but that wasn't how I felt at all. I couldn't take my eyes off her. I just focused on her, as if she was the only one on stage. I felt as if she was dancing just for me. I think she was. I can remember the exact moment when I thought that. I sat in the audience smiling all night. That wasn't something I'd bragged about to Tom and the others, either. After the concert she'd come running up to me, full of herself, and I decided then to tell her.

'I've got something to tell you,' I'd started off, daring, and she had swirled away from me and back again.

'And I've got something to tell you,' she had said. 'The Head of Sixth Form wants me to do A level Dance. No one's ever taken it in our school before!'

She had swirled off then, as excited as a little kid, and I caught her excitement and started dancing after her, making out I was all long legs and big feet and elbows poking out all over the place. I was laughing out loud, and so was she.

'What did you want to tell me?' she shouted at me.

'I can't remember. It wasn't important.' I remember brushing my hair out of my eyes and grinning at her, teasing. It would keep. I had a feeling that I would have a lot of chances to say it. Besides, for the moment I had no idea whether I'd get the words out without making a fool of myself.

'How many words is it?' she had asked, as cocky as a sparrow.

I told her, 'Three.'

And she had laughed up at me and said, 'Three back, Chris.'

She wasn't in the sixth-form block. Her friend Ruthlyn was there, leaning underneath a portrait of the last headteacher and whistling jauntily. When she saw me she waved and strolled casually over to me, smiling her wide smile, swinging her schoolbag like the pendulum of a clock.

'What's wrong?' I asked.

'What d'you mean, what's wrong?' Ruthlyn's smile broadened. 'Why should anything be wrong?'

'I can tell by your face. Where's Helen?'

'Oh, Helen. She's gone home.'

'She's supposed to be meeting me.'

'She went a bit funny in afternoon registration and Miss Clancy sent her home.'

'What d'you mean, funny?' I tried to keep my voice casual, like Ruthlyn's.

She smiled at me, her eyes shining as if going funny in afternoon registration was the best thing that could possibly have happened to Helen. 'A bit kind of . . .' she waved her hands about and tottered unsteadily. 'You know, like that.'

'Drunk, you mean?'

Ruthlyn laughed loud and easy. She tucked her schoolbag under her arm. 'Just funny. Just a bit funny. So she asked me to give you her love and she'll see you soon.'

'I'll go round there now.' I was worried. Ruthlyn was being infuriating.

'I wouldn't,' she said. 'Leave her a bit.'

'I'll phone her, then.'

She shook her head. 'Wait for her to phone you, she said.'

I wanted to sit down.

'Ruthlyn. What's happening?'

'Tell you what,' she said. 'I'll ask Helen to come round to my house one night, and you come round as well, and you can talk to her there.'

'Tonight?'

'Give her till the weekend. Honest, Chris, she just needs a bit of a rest and then she'll be all right.'

I knew she was feeling sorry for me. I wished she wouldn't. My breath wasn't coming right, for some reason. Up till last weekend Helen and I had seen each other every day for months. 'I suppose you're allowed to go round and see her? I mean, you haven't got leprosy or bad socks or whatever it is they've all got against me at her house?'

'I'll go round tonight,' said Ruthlyn. 'See you, Chris.' We had reached the corner of the road where she lived. One of her little brothers ran up to her and, laughing, she scooped him up. 'Oi. Chris!' she shouted, as I walked away. 'Catch!' She threw me a small packet.

I opened it as soon as I had gone round the corner. It was a book of love sonnets by a Victorian poet called Elizabeth Barrett Browning. 'Happy Valentine's Day,' it said inside. 'From Helen.'

I'd been to Ruthlyn's quite often before, usually to family parties. They had always been colourful occasions with loud music and wonderful Jamaican food. Ruthlyn's mother was a friendly giant of a woman called Coral. Her voice was as steamy as hot treacle. Ruthlyn and all the little ones speak broad Sheffield, but Coral's accent is pure Jamaica. I think she must be a great mother to have; she's so warm and kind. She never stops talking, though, or singing, when she's in the mood.

'Here come the spidah!' she said when she opened the door to me on that Saturday. 'When you goin' to hang some fat on those bones of yours, hey? When you goin' to fill out and be a muscle-man?'

'Is Helen here?' I looked round, anxious. The house was full of grinning children, all with their faces turned up towards me.

'Oh, she in with Ruthlyn. They full of secrets, I'm telling you!'

'They always are.' I ran up to Ruthlyn's room three steps at a time, eager to see Helen again. I hesitated for a second outside the door, then tapped on it and went in. The two girls stopped talking at once. It was obvious that Helen had been crying. Her face was white and strained. I stopped in the doorway, uncertain.

'Are you better?' I asked.

Ruthlyn stood up. 'I'll go and make some coffees.'

'I hate coffee,' said Helen. 'It tastes like potato peel.'

Ruthlyn closed the door behind her, and I immediately went over to Helen and sat on the arm of her chair. She wouldn't look at me, and I didn't know what to say to her. She was leaning back, her mouth slightly open, her eyes closed tight. I'd never seen her looking so ill and tired. I took her hand, and she let it lie in mine, limp and cold.

'What's up with you?' I said. 'Is it flu?'

She shook her head. Tears oozed slowly from her closed lids, and she didn't try to stop them. I watched them ooze and ooze again, tired and slow, little languid trails that would never stop. She didn't make a sound. I could feel my heart beginning to lurch like the insistent beating of a drum, a slow and sickening lurch. My limbs felt heavy with dread. I remembered my dream again. I remembered the crack in the ice between us, opening out to drift us apart. I took Helen's other hand and held them both in my own. I felt as if I was trying to warm them into life.

'Helen. What is it?'

And she answered me in a hollow, frightened, weary voice that I would hardly have recognized as hers, and that I'll never forget in my life.

* * *

February 27th

Dear Nobody,

At home there's a tap in the bathroom that won't turn off properly. It needs a new valve, that's all, Mum says. Sometimes you don't hear it at all, and sometimes it keeps you awake all night, drip, drip, drip, regular and slow and insistent.

And that's how I feel about you.

It's like hearing my own heartbeat and not being able to switch it off.

It's like footsteps in the dark.

I don't know whether you're there at all.

But the thought that you might be there is like a drip, drip, drip that won't go away, day and night, day and night now, regular and slow and insistent, like a beating pulse that won't lie still, like a clock that never stops ticking.

Pregnant, pregnant, what if I'm pregnant? Tick tock tick tock tick . . .

I'm so frightened at night that I can hardly breathe.

I can't tell anyone. I can't tell Ruthlyn. I can't tell Mum.

You're only a shadow. You're only a whisper.

You're a tap, dripping night and day.

But I've told Chris, at last, at last. Perhaps that will make you go away.

Leave me alone.

I don't want you.

Go away. Please, please, go away.

★ ★ ★

That was the first of Helen's Dear Nobody letters, and reading it was like opening the door on a nightmare.

March

It would be difficult to describe the feelings that rushed through my mind that evening in February – shock, surprise, disbelief, and an overwhelming feeling of relief that Helen wasn't ill, and that she hadn't gone off me, or anything. I didn't believe what she had told me but I felt closer to her than I'd ever felt before, responsible and protective. Later on I felt terrible. I sat holding her hand while Ruthlyn brought in a tray of coffees and milk and toast. Her chattering floated over us as I stroked Helen's hair, noticing how the light shone in it, and how soft it was; I willed Ruthlyn to go away and leave us alone together.

We walked back to Helen's house in silence, so full of thoughts that there was nothing to say. I had my arm round her. 'It'll be all right,' I kept saying. 'I'll stay with you, whatever happens.' The words just came out. I've no idea what I meant by them. When I thought about them afterwards I went cold and scared inside, but at the time it seemed to be the only thing to say, so I said it. I couldn't really believe that it was true, but I did feel desperately sorry for Helen because she was so obviously unhappy. I would have done anything to make her feel better.

When we reached her door Helen drew away from me and I tried to make her stay out a little longer. I didn't want to let her go, and I didn't want to be left alone with my bewildered thoughts. Clouds slid across the moon like great winged birds, hiding and showing its light, hiding and showing Helen's face. She looked so young.

'I won't ask you in,' she said.

'No. I don't want to come in. I don't want to go away from you, either.'

'I was horrible to you,' she said. 'I'm sorry. I was frightened. I didn't know what to say to you.'

'I was frightened, too. I thought you wanted to finish with me.'

'Oh, Chris!'

It was difficult to talk after that. We were only just aware of lights being turned on and off in the house, the bath being emptied, someone coming down the stairs.

'I'd better go in,' Helen said. Her voice was stricken. I hated to leave her like that.

'You're probably mistaken about it. It might be just worry. It's too soon to know, isn't it?'

'I don't know. I just don't know.'

'I wish I'd been more careful . . .'

'Not just you. It was my fault, too.'

'We were so stupid! It's not as if we're a pair of kids.'

The door was opened. Helen's mother put two milk bottles on the step. 'I don't like this hanging round doorways,' she said. 'I've told you that, Helen.'

And Helen ran in, too upset to say goodnight to me.

The next two days, before she rang again, were like a prison sentence. I daren't leave the house in case she rang when I was out. I daren't ring her house or go round. I spent hours sitting on the stairs by the phone, pretending to read, pretending to comb my hair in the mirror, stroking the cat, anything. Dad watched me and said nothing. I don't suppose I was much worth talking to at the time. Our phone gives a little burp just when it's about to ring. When I heard it at last I snatched it up, knowing it would be her, not wanting anyone else to speak to her before I did.

'Any news?' I asked.

'Not yet,' she told me. 'But Mum thinks I'm anaemic.'

'What can you do about that?'

'Well, I could eat loads of prunes or I could go to the doctor for some iron tablets. So I'm going to see the doctor tonight.'

'Can I meet you after?'

'All right.'

I walked up to the health centre near Helen's house and sat on the wall waiting for her. A man was crossing the road from the library with a little group of kids; he was carrying one in his arms and clutching the hand of another one, and two others clung on to the side of his coat. They were all carrying library books, all chattering their heads off at once like a nestful of birds. He looked as if he could do with a shave. I found myself daydreaming that Helen had quads and that I took them everywhere with me. I was on television as the youngest father of quads. The baby dropped her book over the man's shoulder and started screaming, and he shouted at the youngest child for not picking it up. She sat on the pavement and howled. One of the other two fell over her and they all screamed then. I switched off my daydream and jumped off the wall to meet Helen.

'Is it all right?' I asked, and she nodded and took my hand. The doctor had given her a prescription and had told her that lots of girls of her age needed extra iron. 'She said we live life too fast and we get run down easily. She asked about my A levels and about you.'

'About me?'

'Well, she asked if I had a steady boyfriend and I said

yes, and she asked if I needed to talk about anything to do with my relationship with you, and I said no.'

'Maybe you should have, just to put your mind at rest.'

'How could I? It would go on my records, wouldn't it? Just supposing my mum came into the surgery with me one day, she'd only have to look at my records to find out. So she gave me these leaflets about family planning and said I mustn't ever feel shy about talking to her or asking her anything. She was really nice.'

'And you think you're okay?'

'I think so. I feel tons better just for seeing her.'

'You look it. We've been lucky, then.'

'I know. We mustn't take chances like that again.'

It's amazing what you can kid yourself into believing, if you really want to. We were silly with happiness that evening, telling jokes and laughing loud enough to scare ghosts away. They creep back though, don't they?

I didn't see Helen again till the end of the week. Though I rang every day she always answered the phone briefly, in low monosyllables, so I was aware that her mother was probably in the house and she couldn't talk freely. I always asked her if she was all right and she always said, 'I don't know.'

'What do you mean, you don't know? The doctor said, didn't she . . . ?'

'Nothing's changed, Chris. That's what I mean.'

I didn't know what to do with myself. It was as if everywhere I looked huge black flapping birds were casting their shadows, ruffling the air round me with their billowy wingbeats, peering down at me with their sharp beaky faces and angry eyes. I couldn't talk to anyone about it. I sat watching my dad at night, pulling his lip the way he does when the news is on, and I knew I wouldn't even know where to start. I didn't even know if it was true. In a desperate sort of way I wanted to bury my head in my mother's side like I did when I was a little kid with sore knees, and when I thought about that I wanted to shout out, because even that memory had been smothered somewhere, in my pillow probably, eight years ago. It was as if it had risen from nowhere to make me a child again. I was angry with her. Of all people she should have been there. She should have been there to talk to. And even as I thought that, I stood staring out of the window with my fists clenched tight in my pockets, trying to imagine how I would tell my mother if she was there, and what she would say to me about it all. I couldn't imagine it. Where on earth do the words come from?

One afternoon Tom told me he was going to the climbing wall at the Poly and asked me if I fancied going with him. I think even he could tell I was screwed up about something. So I said I'd go, mostly because all of a sudden it seemed like a lead-in to getting in touch with my mother again after all. It would be something to tell her, I supposed, that I'd started climbing. Maybe she'd write back to me with some tips. 'Hold tight, Christopher!' I'd never even heard of the climbing wall before, but I reckoned it would be a bit easier than dangling off Stanage Edge in front of all the hard climbers of Derbyshire and Yorkshire. It would be a way of finding out a little bit more about Mum.

It was hot and sweaty in there. Students stood, or squatted on their haunches, in small groups, flexing out their fingers as though they were practising on invisible musical instruments. The wall rose steeply up away from us, with lots of jutting ledges lower down, though they seemed to get fewer and smaller the higher up it went. Still, it looked easy enough. I was surprised at how cautious some of the climbers were.

'How d'you fancy it, Chris?' Tom asked me. 'Reckon we'll get to the top?'

'After you, Tom-boy,' I said.

He swung up the thing like a spider while I clung with sickening swirls of my stomach to the plastic rock, my fists clenched into holes, my knees dithering. Thank goodness Helen wasn't there to see me, that's all I can say.

When I next saw Helen she was on her own, walking down Ecclesall Road with her hands in her pockets, daydreaming. She didn't even see me at first. It always gives me a kick, seeing her unexpectedly like that.

'Helen!' I shouted. I dodged between the traffic to get to her side of the road and walked along with her.

'I'm going to Grandad's,' she told me.

'I'll come with you,' I said. I like her grandfather. He talks to you dead straight, and I respect that in people. Her grandmother's strange, though. I don't think I've ever managed to get a word out of her, but she's got that way of staring at you, like Helen's mother has sometimes, staring at you without saying anything, making you feel raw.

'I think I'll go on my own,' she said.

I shrugged. 'Okay. I don't mind.' But I did mind. I didn't want to share her with anyone just then, not even with her grandad.

'Are you all right, though?' I asked her.

She dug her hands deep in her pockets again, and I put my arm round her, as if by keeping her warm I could do something about the dread that was spreading like a cold fog inside me.

'I'm all right,' she said. 'Nothing's changed, Chris.'

★ ★ ★

Dear Nobody,
   Nothing has changed.

The tap still drips, night after sleepless night.

What if I'm what if what what if I'm

I had one glorious day with Chris, when we seemed to be able to make the ticking stop.

But nothing had changed. Nothing.

There's a little frightened pulse beating inside me, deep deep down.

Go away go away go away.

There's nobody there.

Please don't be there.

Today when I got up I looked at myself in the mirror. My face was grey. I've got dark rings under my eyes from not sleeping. I don't know myself. Where've I gone?

I put on my favourite dress. I took it off and threw it on the floor, then I sat on my bed, gripping my hands and listening to the ticking inside me and looking across at this grey-faced creature with huge black eyes. My room's a tip. I haven't tidied it for days. My clothes are dumped round the floor like little molehills coming through the carpet. There's a mug of tea with green slime on it. I don't know myself. I feel desperately alone.

I decided to go and see Grandad. Sometimes I think he's my best friend. When I was little I used to save up all my sadnesses to tell him. He would sit me on a stool in the kitchen and crouch down in front of me and listen solemnly, all the way through. When I'd finished telling them I felt better. It was just the fact that he spared the time to listen, I think; took me seriously, even when I was only a few years old. So I felt that perhaps I could tell Grandad, and he would understand. I met Chris on the way there. He wanted to come with me, but I told him I needed to be on my own. There was no way I could have told Grandad if Chris had been there. I don't think Chris understood, but that's not my fault.

Grandad was cooking tea when I arrived – fried eggs and chips. The smell of it made me feel a bit sick. I asked him for a drink of water.

'Are you all right, Helen?' he asked me.

I perched myself on the kitchen stool and watched him. He scooped hot oil over the eggs. He counted under his breath – three scoops for each egg. The oil sizzled round the yolks, the white thickened. He glanced up at me.

'You look a bit off colour.'

It was my cue, and I couldn't take it. I smiled back at him over my glass, and though he kept on looking at me in that questioning way he has, that usually would make me put my arms round him and blurt everything out, he said nothing more, and neither did I. He turned back to his cooking, whistling something without a tune, and when the meal was cooked I followed him upstairs to see Nan.

She stays in her room most of the time, and it's always dark and stuffy in there. I long to open the windows wide and pull back the curtains, let them flap and drift. Everything is so still, as if the clocks have all stopped a long time ago. I chatted away to her about Robbie and school, and she tucked into her food and nodded occasionally. She doesn't listen, though. I think she's locked in some kind of daydream world that she'd rather be in. I wonder what she thinks about. I had a wild urge to say to her, 'Nan, I think I might be pregnant,' and I think she'd have carried on nodding and sucking vinegar off her chips and not heard a word of it. Perhaps I should have said it. At least I would have given a voice to my nightmare. But I didn't. Grandad had gone out to see a film by the time I left, and I caught a bus home, feeling wretched, feeling sick with worry. There was no one I could talk to.

So today I went to the Family Planning Clinic.

I thought I would ask Ruthlyn to go with me but in the end I didn't. I just can't bring myself to tell her. You imagine you'll tell your best friend when something like this happens to you but when it comes to it you can't. You can't tell anyone. She guesses, I'm sure she does, but she's too discreet to ask me outright and I'm too ashamed and nervous to tell her.

So I went to the Family Planning Clinic on my own and

as soon as I went into the reception room and saw all those young women sitting there, most of them smoking, most of them looking fed up and tired and lonely, I knew I couldn't stay. I felt desperate inside.

I pretended I was looking for someone who wasn't there and then I just walked out and caught the bus home.

I'm so frightened. I feel as if I'm walking through a wilderness. There's nothing to hold on to.

Go away. Please go away.

★ ★ ★

Dear Joan,

I'm just having a breather after a session at the climbing wall at the Poly. I haven't got any of the proper gear yet but when I'm a student (next year, I'm going to Newcastle University to do an English degree, did I tell you?) I think I'll be able to borrow ropes and a helmet and stuff there. You must tell me about some of your expeditions some time. I could do with some tips. It's a wonderful hobby, isn't it? I've only just started so I can't call it a hobby yet (in fact I haven't quite got to the top of the wall yet but I can see how to do it. I twisted my ankle a bit because I came down a bit fast, but when it's better I think I'll get to the top easily). I think climbing must be in my blood. Did you climb in Derbyshire when you lived down here? I expect you climb in the Lake

District now, or Scotland. Maybe I'll come up there to do some when I'm more experienced and you could show me the ropes! Joking apart, I would like to pop in to see you some time.

Your son,

Christopher

I had to wait round for hours at the climbing wall while Tom shinned up and down the thing, bragging at the top of his voice. My ankle was hurting and my fingers were sore, and my knees felt like balloons. I wrote a letter to my mother. I felt it had just the right tone, not pretending I was an expert climber yet, but showing her that we have got something in common and opening things out for her to write back to me. I put it back in my schoolbag and waited for Tom to come off the wall.

'You all right?' he shouted at me when he'd finished at last. Of course everybody had to look at me.

'Course,' I said. 'It was great, that. Classic.'

'You didn't stay on long.'

'I remembered I had an important letter to write.'

He grinned. Old Tom. He thinks he's the handsomest devil alive but you should see his teeth when he grins.

'Coming for a jar?' he asked me.

'Just one,' I said. 'I've got a timed essay to do tonight.'

'Haven't we all,' said Tom. '"Hamlet could do with a pint of Heineken. Discuss."'

I hobbled after him to the pub and sat with my head down and my hands clasping the glass on my knees as if I was trying to heat the stuff up. The noise of the place swirled round me. I felt as if I was drowning in it. I wanted to think about Helen. What was she doing now? What was happening to her? Those angry-eyed birds glared down at me, peering from the shadows. I wanted to go home.

'I wish you'd shut up,' Tom said. 'I can't get a word in edgeways.'

I shrugged. The pub was full of noisy people, laughing, talking too loud, pushing against each other. It reminded me of a cattle stall over at Hope market. If you thought about it too much, it even smelt like it.

'I'm going cycling in France this summer,' Tom said. 'Don't fancy coming, do you?'

I shook my head.

'We always said we'd do it after the As. You're fit enough, aren't you?'

'Haven't done any long distance since we did the Dales.'

'Plenty of time to work up to it. Do a long run every weekend.'

I sighed and shook my head. It would mean four weeks away from Helen.

'France, though!' Tom leaned forward, raising his glass a little like a toast. '*La belle France!* Baguettes at dawn! Say you'll come! It'll be miserable on my own. I'll go anyway, but it won't be the same.'

I leaned back in my bench. France! We'd always said we'd do it, he was right, before we went off to university.

'You were dead keen before the mocks, Chris.'

'I've gone off it, that's all.'

Maybe Helen would come out with Ruthlyn and camp in Brittany and we could travel there and back with them. What's it like, camping when you're six months' pregnant? What's it like, being pregnant?

'Wake up,' said Tom.

'I was just thinking,' I said. 'What if Hamlet had got Ophelia pregnant?'

'Bloody hell!' said Tom. He drained back his glass of beer and stared at me, froth clinging like a moustache to his top lip. 'Bloody hell, Chris!'

★ ★ ★

March 22nd

Dear Nobody,

I bought a home pregnancy test today. I was sick again

this morning. You are an alien growth in me. You are a disease. I want you not to exist.

I have to know.

I stayed off school till mid-morning. Mum and Dad were both out at work. I wish I could have asked Ruthlyn to buy the kit for me but I just didn't have the courage. I went to Boots in town where I wouldn't be recognized, and stood dithering by the counter and looking away and wondering about buying throat pastilles instead, and then, of all things, I was served by a male assistant. He didn't even look at me. Maybe he was embarrassed too, or maybe he's bored stiff of selling these things to scared schoolgirls. I wore make-up, which I never do because it makes my face itch. I pinched it out of Mum's room. I wanted to look grown-up, but when I saw myself in the mirror in Boots I looked ghastly, deathly white under orange daubs. I went home on the bus clutching my little parcel as if I was scared that someone was going to mug me and run off with it.

The house was so quiet. I took the parcel up to my room and drew the curtain. The kit consisted of a tray and a plastic stopper with some liquid in and a little test tube and a dipper thing that looked like a swizzle stick for a cocktail. It should have had one of those paper umbrellas on the top. Everything was in miniature, like a child's toy chemistry set. I had to pour the liquid from the plastic bag thing into the test tube and immediately it went bright purple. Something like giggles kept popping out of me, only I don't think I was laughing. Actually, I think I was crying. Aloud, you know, in little loud hiccupping bursts. My hands were dithering so much that it's a wonder I didn't spill everything over the carpet. But I did it, somehow I managed to read the instructions and hold things the right way up and do it. Then I had to wait five minutes.

Have you any idea how long five minutes last? The silence in the house while I sat looking at my watch was like that deathly quiet you get in a three-hour exam, I swear it. Three hours when you read and read the questions and you don't know any of the answers. I tried to think of all the things people would be doing during that time. Mum would be typing away on her computer keyboard at the bank. Dad would be filing books away, humming a jazz tune to himself in his quiet library. Grandad would be making himself a cup of tea, stirring and stirring the leaves in his teapot the way he does, peering down into its steam. Ruthlyn would be in Maths, where I should be. And Chris. What were you doing then, Chris, while my test tube was concocting its brew? Were you thinking about me?

And when I took the cocktail swizzle stick out it wasn't

pink at the end. It was white. I read the instructions again. If the end is pink, you are pregnant. If it is white, you are not pregnant. I'm not pregnant. You don't exist.

You are nobody.

Dear Nobody,

Later.

After I'd done that pregnancy test I went to the music centre to work, just as if it was an ordinary day. Well, it was, after all. I had to do some work on a Bach mass. I love that music. I love all kinds of way-out music and I suppose Bach is way-out for people of my age to like, too. It just bursts in my head, all the time, when I've been working on it. I looked through some of the music scores and found myself reading composers' names out loud. I'd never realized before how beautiful they sound. Stravinsky. Vivaldi. Delius. No wonder they write glorious music when they've got names like that. How can I ever hope to be a composer with a name like Garton? I looked in the Gs in the index to see if there was a Garton there and I found Gluck. Fancy having a name like Gluck. It sounds more like something going down the plughole. Gluck Gluck Gluck, I said aloud, and all the music students looked up at me and frowned.

I felt great.

I ran home with my head all full of music and had a fight with Robbie at teatime because he reckoned he was always going to have my tea. But I'd decided I was hungry again. Mum just sat back in her chair in the kitchen and let us get on with it. She looked really tired. I've been so obsessed with myself lately that I haven't taken any notice of anyone else. I wonder what her private thoughts are, if she has sensed what I've been going through. How hard it would have been to tell her. I just wouldn't have known where to start. I wish I could talk to her. I haven't been able to since I was a little girl, I don't know why. I don't think she loves me as much now that I'm grown-up. Sometimes I think she'd like me to be a little girl again, to make pretty clothes for and cuddle at bedtime. She doesn't really know me any more.

As soon as I could I went to Chris's house. I couldn't wait to see him. I wanted to tell him it was all right, and that the wheels of the world had started turning again. He wasn't in, after all, but I'd loved the walk there down all the fresh rainy streets.

'You all right?' said Chris's father. 'You're looking pasty.'

'I'm fine. Tell Chris I'm fine.'

'Come on in and wait for a bit,' he said. 'He mightn't be long. He's playing on a climbing frame or something.'

I really like Chris's dad. I can never tell whether he's pulling my leg or not, some of the things he says.

'I was just going to switch off the kiln. Want to have a look down the grotto?'

I followed him down the narrow cellar steps that led to his pottery room. The shelves were lined with cups and bowls and vases waiting to be glazed, and there were stacks of ice-cream cartons with interesting words on the labels. Grog and Dolomite, Wood-ash. Ochre. I let the names roll in my head. It was hot and stuffy down there. He switched off his kiln, and the low buzzing sound that I'd been aware of stopped.

'Can I see in the kiln?' I asked.

'Much too hot,' he told me. 'I'll have to leave it a day before I open that door. Have a look at these. I took them out the other day.' He slid a tray of mugs from a shelf. 'Look at that,' he said, pleased. 'Aren't they grand! Just right.'

He handled his cups lovingly, holding them up to the light so I could see the oyster-shell pattern on the base. I'd never thought of cups as works of art. They're just useful containers.

'It's lovely stuff, clay,' he told me. I think he's a bit obsessed with the stuff. I think you'd have to be, to mess about with it all day. Perhaps that's where the word 'potty' comes from. 'Have you never worked it? It's like breadmaking, only faster. It's slippery as fishes when you get it going, and you've got to get it just right or it sinks in your hands into a wet mess. Have a go. Here, while you're waiting. Have a go.'

He sat me on a stool in front of some clay, and set a pail of water by me. 'Just play with it,' he said. 'Get used to the texture, that's the thing.'

He set his wheel going and dumped a lump of clay on to the centre of it. He hollowed it out with his thumbs and then kept slipping water over it while he bulged the sides up fast with the crooks of his fingers. 'Got a memory, clay has,' he told me. 'Once you've got it going one way, it'll always go that way. Bit like me!' he laughed. 'Stubborn.' The stuff was fluid under his big fingers, solid and liquid at the same time. It was like living water. I couldn't take my eyes off it.

'Don't be scared of it, that's the thing,' he said. 'Try it.' There was a kind of chanting going on in my head. I tried to close it out. I rolled my piece of clay; I loved the way it slithered in my fingers. I tried to shape it into a ball, then dug in my thumbs to make a hole, and at the same time I was pinching the base to make it bell out. I was totally absorbed in this. It hollowed out like a cave. I put it down on the ledge. The chanting wouldn't go away. I picked up a small blob of clay and began to shape it. I didn't know what I was doing. I made a tiny doll, without even thinking about it. It was like the little plasticine models I used to make at infant school. It had a tiny head and a little round fat body. It was so small I could hold it in my palm and curl my hand over it. I dropped the little round body into the hollow cave I'd made, then swiftly, swiftly in case Mr Marshall had seen me, I dipped and wet the top so that the lips of the cave met like a mermaid's purse. I nursed it in my hands, shaping it and smoothing it.

'What's that you're making?' Mr Marshall laughed. 'An Easter egg, is it?'

'Something like that,' I said. It was as if he'd woken me up from a deep sleep. I put the egg down and let it roll on the table. I felt myself growing hot all over. Pins of heat like scratches prickled my skin. The air was black around me. Somewhere under a black sea a voice boomed. I was in a hot ocean, and my arms and my legs were lumbering things, sliding out and down, and my head was an enormous cave, and still the voice boomed, and then turned silver-thin and went out.

When I came round I was sitting by the open door of the cellar, with the night air cold on me and Chris's dad kneeling by me. He was holding my hand.

'I forget how stuffy it gets down here sometimes,' he said. 'You frightened the life out of me, the way you keeled over then. You sit there till you're better. I'll bring a rug down to put round you.'

'I'm sorry,' I said. I was cold all over.

'Don't be soft. Sorry! I've seen big strong men faint in my time, soldiers even, in the heat. Passing-out parade they call it, and they're all passing out, dropping like flies in the heat. You'll be fine in a jiffy. I'll ring your dad to come and pick you up in a bit.'

'No. Don't do that!' I said. Mr Marshall gave me an odd look then. He must have heard panic in my voice, or something.

'His band's playing at the Ringinglow tonight,' I added. I wasn't sure whether that was true or not. I couldn't remember what day it was, even. 'I'll be fine in a minute. I feel better already.'

Mr Marshall made me some tea and we waited a little for Chris to come back. I just wanted to go to bed. Mr Marshall walked with me to the corner of our road and then I just ran home and straight to my room. I wanted to howl.

You don't exist.

You're nobody.

So why? Why?

★ ★ ★

I had another letter to my mother in my pocket. When I read through the last one it sounded as if a seven-year-old had written it. I walked home in the pouring rain, mouthing the words of the new letter, wondering whether I'd have the courage to actually send it, whether it was worth the effort even, when I saw my Aunty Jill arriving at our house and Dad letting her in. I ran into the house just as Dad was closing the door and shook myself like a dog in the hall, wanting to annoy them for some reason.

'Could have done with you half an hour ago,' Dad told me. 'Your Helen was here. She fainted down in the cellar. I'm not surprised, stuffy little hole it is.'

'I'll go round and see her,' I said.

'Do no such thing,' Dad told me. 'She's as right as rain, but I told her to get an early night. No point waking her up, Chris.'

'She's a nice girl, Helen,' Jill said. 'You'll miss her when you go away.'

'I know,' I said. My insides had gone as fidgety as an anthill. I didn't want to stand in the hall chatting. I wanted to see Helen.

Dad shrugged. 'Who can tell, at their age? They think the world of each other, those two. Too young to get tied down, though, Chris.'

'I know. I know that. I'm not daft,' I said. I went into the kitchen to put the kettle on. Anything to get away from them both, grinning away at me as if having a girlfriend was like winning a ribbon on sports day. 'Did she come round for any reason?' I asked, as casually as possible.

'Aye. She came to tell you she was fine,' Dad laughed.

I closed my eyes. I leaned my head against the tiled wall.

'She looked fine as well, white as a ghost down there.'

'She's had flu,' I said. 'Something like that.'

'She told me she's doing Dance for one of her exams,' Dad said. 'Funny subject, that.'

'No funnier than Greek,' Jill said. 'And that's what I did. Look where that got me. Three kids and a field of horses.'

Their voices buzzed behind me in the hall.

'Fancy a drink?' Dad asked her.

'What d'you think I've come for? The nine o'clock news?'

It was good to get rid of them. As soon as the door closed behind them I put a cassette on really loud. The whole house was vibrating with the noise. Guy screeched at me to pack it in. I didn't care. I opened all the windows wide. I wanted the music to throb down all the way to Helen's house. She's fine. Nothing's wrong.

* * *

Dear Nobody,

Yesterday evening I bought another pregnancy test. This

time I read the instructions properly. It had to be done first thing. This morning I shut myself in my room. Mum was in the kitchen downstairs, singing loudly to some jazz on the radio. She was in one of her rare happy moods. I think maybe when I was little she used to sing a lot. I don't really remember. Most of the time she's locked up in her own thoughts, like my nan. They don't seem to like each other much, my mum and her mum. They hardly ever see each other. I hope it doesn't ever get that bad between Mum and me. I'd hate that.

'I'll tell her,' I promised myself. 'Whatever it says, I'll tell her.' My hands were shaking as I dipped the plastic stick in the test tube. I sat on my bed and waited. I didn't care if Mum came into the room and saw me. I lifted out the stick, but I knew before I looked at it what colour it would be. Pink. Positive. Thursday negative. Saturday positive.

The phone rang. Mum was still singing. She didn't hear it. I let it ring and ring. It seemed to be a voice from another planet, trying to make contact with Earth. At last Robbie pounded down the stairs and answered it. 'Helen!' he shouted up the stairs. 'It's for you.' I didn't move.

Robbie put the phone down and went back to his room. He turned on his music, loud, to drown out Mum's singing. I emptied the test glass down the lavatory and put the plastic tray and spatula and stuff in my drawer. I washed my face and brushed my hair, and then I went down to Mum. I was going to tell her.

Mum looked round at me when I went into the kitchen. She must have been able to tell that I was upset.

'There you are. I thought you were still asleep. I'm making a pie for tea. D'you fancy making the pastry? Your pastry's always better than mine.'

I would tell her everything and she would hold me and stroke me like she did when I was a little girl. She would make me better. She would sticking-plaster my hurts and make them go away. She ought to know. Of all the people in the world she ought to know.

I fetched flour and lard and butter from the larder and set them out on the work surface. I was hollow inside. I felt as if I was doing everything in slow motion. Words were lining themselves up like soldiers in my head. Mum stood back to take a top note, lifting herself up on her toes, making fun of herself.

'You should join a choir, Mum,' I began. I should have gone straight into it. I was in a trap now. 'You've got a really good voice.'

'D'you think so? I don't know how to read music though, that's my trouble.'

'Get Dad to teach you.'

'Ted! He couldn't teach a frog to leap, that man.'

Do it! Do it! Get it over with.

I took a deep breath. 'Mum,' I began. 'I want to tell you something.'

The music programme on the radio finished and turned into cricket scores. Mum clucked and turned the knob. All the sounds distorted. Robbie burst into the kitchen.

'Helen, you moron! I was shouting for you for ages. Chris rang up about half an hour ago. He said if you come in he wants to meet you in the park at twelve.'

'I'm helping Mum,' I said. I felt like crying. The radio sounds howled and stuttered.

Mum took the bag of flour from my hand and tipped some on to the scales. 'Off you go, young lady,' she said. 'I thought you and Chris had had a row, the way you've been behaving. Go and make it up with him.'

'Mum . . .'

'Off you go, Helen.'

I turned away and then I went back to my mum. I put my arms round her and put my head on her shoulder. She laughed with surprise and tried to ease me away. I wanted her to rock me. I wanted her to hold me tight. I didn't want to let go.

'What's all this about?' she asked me.

'Yuk!' Robbie said.

Then Mum moved away. 'This'll never get the meal

cooked,' she said. 'Off you go. Don't keep the young man waiting.'

Chris was sitting on a small wooden roundabout in the kiddies' playground, letting his heels drag as it revolved. He had his head bent and didn't see me as I went up to him, so the roundabout had to do another revolution before it came back to me again. It gave me time to think my script out.

'Chris!' I said.

He jumped off at once. 'Don't talk,' he said. 'Let me just hold you. I've missed you. It's been days and days.'

'I wanted to talk to my mum,' I told him. 'And I couldn't.'

'Let's just be together,' he said. 'Don't talk yet.'

We walked over to the little river that ran through the park. We came to the shadows of the trees. Lovely trees. I stroked their rough trunks. I needed their solidness. Lovely friendly trees. Imagine living in a country without trees.

'What's the matter?' Chris asked me.

'I did a test,' I told him. 'And it was negative. Then I fainted at your dad's. I did another test this morning. And it was positive.'

I felt stronger when I'd told him, though I couldn't let go of the tree, not yet. I was talking with my cheek pressed against it. I was abstracted from myself. Someone else was doing the talking. 'How can something be negative and positive? How can it be and not be?'

There is a huge mystery in me that's too deep and frightening to be solved.

'I don't understand,' I said.

'Neither do I,' said Chris. 'I won't leave you, Nell. You know that. I love you.'

It was as if he couldn't think of anything else to say.

* * *

After I left Helen I started to run back home. I was numb. A baby is. A baby's not. Something and nothing. Somebody and nobody. Now and forever. Life began three thousand six hundred million years ago. Life began in January. And I was the father. I tried to wake myself up to the sound of that word, and I couldn't. It was meaningless. It meant I was responsible. It meant Newcastle slipping away from me like a vanishing dream. I felt like a mouse crouching into a tiny hole. I felt the mousy air suffocating me.

We'll be all right. Whatever happens. I won't leave you. I jogged steadily on, forcing my breathing into a rhythm, letting the words bounce with every step I took, flinging my legs forward, head back, fists tight and clenched up.

Whatever happens. I won't leave you. Helen, oh Helen, what have we done? I ran for miles that afternoon.

And then I couldn't sleep. At two in the morning I saw something blazing up in the sky across the oblong of my window. It looked as if it were set on destroying the planet; it seemed to be streaking towards Earth, shimmering and huge among the other stars, a shark among fishes. As I watched it, lying on my back with my arms folded under my head, it rose up and up into the centre of the window, then seemed to veer off to the side and soon streaked out of sight completely. I wished Helen was there with me, making sense of it, making sense of space and making sense of life.

I went into Guy's room and woke him up.

'I've just seen a massive comet,' I told him.

He sat up for a second. 'It was a plane,' he said. Then he flopped back on his pillow like a dead man, fast asleep.

* * *

March 30th

Dear Nobody,

Last night I decided what I must do. I don't ask your forgiveness for this.

You didn't ask my permission to plant yourself in me, after all. You're like one of those sycamore trees that keep sprouting up from nowhere in our garden. Mum always tugs them out. 'We don't want you here,' she says.

I know just what she means.

I asked Dad if I could borrow the car, as it's Saturday. I told him I wanted to go riding. Robbie wanted to come too, but when he ran upstairs for his tracksuit I drove off without him. I hadn't been riding since I was about twelve. I used to be in love with a great farting steaming stallion called Henry, I remember. I was crazy about him. I used to ride him in my dreams over the moors night after night. Then they sold him because he was too old for hacking, my lovely Henry, and I gave up riding.

So this morning when I woke up after only shreds of sleep I knew what I had to do. I didn't go back to the stables that I used to haunt as a child but drove out ten miles or so from home. When I arrived a ride was about to start, led by a girl not much older than me. They waited for me while I mounted a spare grey, and then walked in file up the road that led on to the moors.

I found myself at the back of the queue. I needed to be at the front for this. I pressed my horse into a trot so I could overtake the others. A woman rider coming out from the stables to join us shouted to me to keep in, and I fell back into place. I should have recognized her, but I didn't. She was quite a way behind. I was staring straight ahead. I was tense and sure of myself, but I wasn't afraid.

I had to get in front. When we crossed the road in file to go through the field gate I let my horse nudge past the others and trotted him on. The girl leader told me Nab had no manners and told him to wait his turn. I ignored her. I turned his head up towards the sheep track that went up the hill and I was shouted back again. The girl trotted up to me and reined in. 'You have to wait for the gate-opener, you know,' she told me. Her face had gone blotchy with embarrassment. I could tell she didn't like to be in charge. 'It's manners,' she said. 'And anyway, I'm the leader. I have to go in front of you all.'

'Sorry,' I said. My eyes were already following the tracks, picking out the shortest route up the hill.

'Don't you know how to rein him in?'

'Course I do.'

'Well, do it then. You'll make the others impatient. Or let him graze for a bit, it won't harm.'

Stubbornly I kept the reins as short as I could, holding myself against Nab's strength as he jerked and tossed his head to try to get his teeth into the juicy young grass. He snorted and stamped, edging his way forward, and I pulled his reins taut till he stood still and calm. As soon as the girl rejoined us he pulled forward. She told me to get to the back. Her face was dark crimson by now.

Anyway, I relaxed. I could already see where I'd be able to break away from the ride. I felt calm.

It was very warm for late March. The heat had brought the midges out already and they danced round the horses, making them snort and toss their heads. The sky was as blue as summers, and there was already a lark up there somewhere. I knew exactly what I had to do. The thoughts in my head were as sharp as ice. I had never felt so sure of anything before.

I was doing it for Chris.

Halfway up the narrow track the leader glanced over her shoulder and sang out, 'Rising trot! Kick them on!' and immediately the horses rose and quickened their pace without being urged by their riders. I dug down into my stirrups. I loved the flow of it, rising and sitting, rising and sitting, the flow and roll of it. I wanted to sing. Then I tensed myself, keen as a bird for my chance. There was a large boulder ahead of us on the path. Beyond that the path split, a slow, twisting track that wound quite gently, and a narrow rabbit-run almost going straight up. I swung Nab towards that one.

'Bring him in!' the girl shouted.

I ignored her.

Come on Nab! Come on Nab! Come on Nab!

Soon I was well in front, and at last had crested the hill. Ahead of me lay a long flat plain studded with young bracken and gorse. The path across it was broad and sandy. I couldn't hear the other riders. I sat straight in my saddle, bracing myself. Now was the time.

I hugged Nab's belly with my knees and my feet. His stride began to lengthen. He held his head high and flung his legs forward, flowing into a canter and then into a full, steady gallop, his hooves thudding a tantivy on the earth. I crouched low now, well into the saddle. I loosened his reins and let him have his head. I was conscious of the firm line of my spine anchoring myself to him. We were one beast, flowing like water through the sharp air. We were one mind. And my stomach rocked like a boat on the tide.

I could hear voices screaming behind me. I kicked Nab on. A shouting voice closed up on me, hooves thundering close behind. I risked a glance over my shoulder and saw the older woman from the stables bearing up on me, lashing her horse forward, and when I looked back again I saw that the hill was sloping down towards a copse. I reared up, trying to rein Nab in. He wouldn't obey.

Now I was panicking. I lost my seat and found myself being flung and thumped about in the saddle, every stride jolting my entire body. My arms and legs flung about, loose and useless. The base of my spine buffeted the saddle again and again. My ribs felt as if they had burst apart. I'd lost the stirrups. I hauled on the reins but Nab jerked himself free; I could see his teeth and his gums bared as he tossed his head. I leaned back as far as I dared, heaving on the reins, and then they slipped out of my fingers. I clung on to the front of the saddle, knotting the hairs of his mane in my fingers. The only thing in my mind was Chris.

I felt the other rider drawing up to me. She was shrieking at me to rein him in. She thundered closer and closer till her horse was brushing right against mine. She leaned across and then she grabbed my reins, and the horses bumped together, jostling for lead, slower now and slower as the woman headed them round from their straight course, and round again, in a tighter and tighter circle, till at last they came to a stop.

I felt as if my skin was loose across my bones. The woman was shouting at me. I slid forward till I was lying with my belly flat across Nab's back. I dropped down and landed on all fours in the heather, and vomited.

The woman swung off her horse and came over to kneel by me. She gave me some tissues to wipe my mouth with.

'Take your hat off,' she said. 'You'll feel cooler.'

I was too weak to do it. She had to undo the chinstrap for me. My hair was damp with sweat.

She eased me up and helped me to walk away to a grassy mound. The sun felt like a blanket, it was so warm and kind. She kept asking me what I'd done it for, and I kept shaking my head. The rest of the party trotted up towards us and she stood up to wave them away. The leader asked if I'd been thrown off, and she told them that I was all right, and that she'd walk back with me.

'You're as white as milk,' she told me. 'But I don't want these horses to get cold. Look how they're steaming. When you're ready we'll go back.'

I said I was ready, but I could hardly stand. My legs juddered as if my knees had been taken away. She helped me over to Nab.

'I don't want to ride.'

'I bet you don't. But if you don't sit on him now you'll never ride a horse again. Just don't puke over him, that's all.'

She cupped her hands together to make a step for me to climb on and heaved me up. I lay across Nab's back, and she helped my legs over and put my feet into the stirrups. 'You *are* in a state,' she said, grim. 'But you'll live.'

We didn't say a word as we walked back. It seemed to take forever. From time to time she glanced over to me, curious, but she didn't say anything. When we reached the house, she told me to go and have a bath. 'You'll be as stiff as a tree tomorrow if you don't,' she told me.

I wanted to be nursed. I would have liked to have been picked up and rocked gently. I wanted to be rocked to sleep. I stood hugging myself while she filled up the bath for me.

'I'm not letting you go home until someone comes for you. I think it should be a doctor, myself.'

'Oh no, please don't.'

'Your dad then. Or Chris.'

I knew who she was, after all. Chris's Aunty Jill. I hadn't wanted to recognize her.

'We're trying to phase out the Aunty bit,' she said. 'After all, he's a big boy now, isn't he?'

That was what I did to you.

Now will you go away?

* * *

The phone call from Aunty Jill woke me up. It must have been midday.

'How's your bike?' she asked, which was an odd question, even for her. I told her about my new Campag. brakes, which didn't impress her much.

'Fancy cycling over here for some lunch?'

'Great.' I was pleased. 'D'you want Guy to come as well?'

'Good heavens, no. I can't manage both of you at once.'

When I arrived she was in the stables, forking out mucky straw and tossing it into a reeking pile in a yard. She came out when she heard me.

'Twenty-eight minutes,' I shouted, swerving up to her.

'I could do it faster by car,' she said.

Then I saw Mr Garton's VW tucked in by the side of the house, and I knew that this wasn't just a casual invitation to lunch.

'What's he doing here?' I asked, cold inside.

She lifted a forkful of new straw from its pile and tossed it into the stable. Gold splinters showered across the yard. 'It's not him. It's Helen. She's having lunch with us.'

'Where is she?'

'She's fast asleep on the settee at the moment. Chris' – as I hopped off my bike and made for the house – 'let her rest for a bit. She's had a bit of a fright. One of the horses bolted with her.'

'Is she all right?'

'She is now. But Chris, before the horse bolted and she lost control she was riding him as if she was in the Grand National. It's a good job I was on Mercury or I'd never have caught up with her. I have to tell you this. She could have killed herself.'

I steadied myself against the shed; leaned back on it and slid down till I was squatting on my haunches.

'Now why should she want to do that?' Jill asked.

I couldn't answer her. I looked towards the house. My throat was a ball, a small spidery ball that hurt and stretched itself and curled up again.

'Something's very wrong, Chris. Am I right?'

My bike was on its side, its wheel still spinning, slower now and slower. I fingered it round again.

'It's something to do with you, as well?'

I nodded. Jill pitched her fork into the straw pile and lifted more into the stable and more again, swinging and lifting and tossing, her dark moving shadow slicing into the bright gold of the pile. She grunted with the effort, lift and swing, lift and swing. Her dark hair swung down across her eyes.

'It's none of my business, and I may have got everything wrong, and forgive me if I have, Chris. But what your Helen did just now up on the moors looked to me like a pretty desperate attempt to get rid of a pregnancy.'

Jill made us some salad. None of us ate much. After we'd eaten she sat on the floor, hugging her knees. Helen and I were sitting side by side on the settee. Jill's front room has a huge wall-window looking out through trees to the paddock where the horses were grazing, and beyond that, to fields and moors. Even though it was warm there were still thin lines of snow threaded under the drystone walls, way up in the distance. We could hear the new leaves rustling just outside the window. The sun danced through them into the room.

'Funny,' Jill said. 'I gave up smoking years ago, and all of a sudden I want a cigarette.' She stretched her arms above her head in a long, tired yawn. 'It's because I want to tell you both something, you know, and it's rather hard.' One of her dogs padded over to her, his paws clicking on the wooden floor, and pushed himself up next to her on her mat. She stroked his long ears. 'I'm going to tell you something that I've never told anyone else. I'm going to keep your secret, by the way. Who you tell, and when and how, is your concern. Look for the good moment to come. And if you want help I'll give it. Okay?' We both nodded. 'I want to tell you something about me. Another secret.'

'I'm full of secrets,' Helen said. 'I'll burst one day. Everyone tells me their secrets at school.'

'Such as?' I asked her, surprised.

'That'd be telling,' Helen smiled. She slipped her shoes off and curled up her legs on the settee, so she was leaning against me, warm and close. Jill, I noticed, had never looked so unsure of herself.

'It was when Ginny was about three, and the boys were at school. I'd really got the stables just started, and it was something I'd always wanted to do. It was the year Mac left me. And the last thing he did was to give me another child.'

'I didn't know . . .' I began. Helen put her hand on my arm. Jill wasn't watching us but was staring out of the windows. The trees were doing a kind of silent dance outside. Their shadows flickered across the floor and the walls.

'And I didn't want the child, you see. I didn't ask for it, and I didn't want it. I couldn't believe it when I found out I was pregnant. At that time it seemed like the worst thing in the world that could happen to me. So I went to the doctor, and he was very sympathetic. I believe I was pretty low, you know, with Mac leaving, and all the worry about the stables. I was shocked and unhappy. And he asked me if I wanted an abortion and I said yes.'

The silence in the room was like something you could touch and hold. Only the dog seemed to be breathing, deep in his sleep. 'He asked me if I was sure and I said yes, yes, absolutely sure, one hundred per cent sure. I do not want this child. And I had the abortion. I didn't tell anyone – not Mac, not my sister, not my mum. No one. I went into hospital on my own and had it done. It was so quick, so easy. When I woke up from the operation I couldn't believe they'd done it. But they promised me they had. They even told me it was a boy. I didn't want to know that. And I came home and I got on with my life.'

The dog shifted and stretched its legs out, slobbering.

'It was as if it had never happened. I got the stables going. And because I hadn't told anyone I had no one to share it with. I felt absolutely alone after that. There was no reason to cry. I didn't have the right to cry. I drove my sadness down so deep that I thought it would never surface again.'

There was a long silence. I would have thought she'd finished speaking, except that she didn't move, or turn her head away from watching the dancing leaves on the window.

She tapped on the floor with her fingers as if she was stubbing out a cigarette. 'He would be nearly fifteen now.'

April

Dear Nobody,

   After all, the good moment for speaking to Mum never came. I was stiff and aching for days but nothing else happened. I told my mum that my horse had bolted and that I had been very shaken. I can't say she was very sympathetic, but then, she doesn't like horses anyway. They make her sneeze, she says. I think she's frightened of them. 'They're very fleshy things, horses,' she said to me one day, with a bit of a shudder, as if that made them nasty or disgusting or rude, even. But I know what she means. It's because they're so physical, so full of muscle and snorting breath, and they're so powerful. She doesn't know what it's like to feel that huge bulk of flesh moving under you, with you. So, when I told her that my horse had bolted, she just sniffed as if to say what did I expect, and left me to get over it. Sometimes I feel as if I'll never get near to my mum again. I want to be able to talk to her about things, the way Ruthlyn talks to her mum, but she doesn't invite it. I think she'd rather not know what's going on in my head. Sometimes when I try to talk to her she just walks away, as if she's slamming a door in my face. How strange it is to think that once I was just that tiny speck of being, moving inside her, just like you in me. Did she want me to be there? I wonder if she was ever close enough to Nan to talk about such things.

I don't know how I got through those few days after my ride on Nab. I'm ashamed. I can't believe what I tried to do out there on the moors. I almost feel as if I was taken over by some mad spirit; some cold, mad other being. I don't know how to talk to Chris about it since that day at Jill's and I know that's hurting him, and he'll be sitting up in his room sad and angry, maybe, and confused, and I wish I could just say to him don't be upset, Chris, just let me work it out for myself, but I can't even bring myself to say that. So I just tell Mum to say that I don't want to speak to him. She probably thinks I've had a row, and maybe that pleased her a little. I'm too young to get serious, she says. What does it mean, to get serious? When I'm with Chris I'm laughing and smiling, we're doing crazy things, all the world's a joke. Well, that's how it used to be, anyway.

But today I sat at the table at lunchtime and refused my food because I just couldn't face it. I'd done that every night this week, I think. This time Mum gave me such a look that I went cold inside, such a strange, quiet, questioning look. She passed my plate over to Robbie without a word and then sent him off to town with Dad to buy trainers. They both grumbled a lot about that, wasting their Saturday afternoon at the shops. Dad and Robbie get on well. I was thinking they'll enjoy it when they get there, and then I realized that I was going to be in the house alone with Mum.

As soon as they went out I ran upstairs to my room. Mum followed me up. She came straight in without knocking and she stood with her hands in her pockets, just watching me, saying nothing, and I knew that this was the moment, right or not. I fumbled wretchedly through the things in my schoolbag, as if somewhere inside it were the words that I needed to say, if only I could fish out the right ones and arrange them in some sort of logical order.

'I want to know what's going on,' she said.

I remember gazing out of the window, and noting somewhere that it was beginning to rain. I could feel a flush creeping across my neck.

'I'm starting a new project,' I told her. 'Miss Clancy said I could start the background work at home.'

'I don't give a damn about Miss Clancy.' My mum closed the door and leaned against it, arms folded now. She was breathing heavily. Her mouth was working as if she had too much saliva to swallow. I could see Chris's photograph grinning at me from my bedside table. He wouldn't come into focus.

'What's going on, Helen?'

My eyes were hurting. Mum's voice wasn't right. She wasn't calm. I looked for the words but I couldn't find them.

'Can't you guess?' I must have been biting my nails – I don't remember doing it, but I do remember Mum leaning forward and slapping my hand away from my mouth. It was an old, familiar gesture from when I was little. It made me feel helpless.

'I can guess,' Mum said, and she leaned back against the door and closed her eyes, and blew out her lips like a fish gasping for air. 'I'd like to have heard it from you, but I can guess,' and her voice was an alien strangled thing in her throat that I didn't recognize. 'How many times have you done it, for goodness' sake?'

It was such a stupid, useless question that it helped me to be angry with her. 'Does it matter?' I shouted at her, and then I was ashamed. She was upset, and it wasn't her fault, none of it was her fault.

'Yes, it does matter, for goodness' sake! It matters to me!'

Mum has sag lines at the corners of her mouth. I could see how the drops of spittle frothed and oozed there, to be wiped away with the back of her hand, to froth and ooze again. And I don't know why but it helped to watch that instead of listening to the way her breath came in snatches, as if she'd torn it off in little pieces. I'd never noticed the hollow in her neck before, and how the skin round it was pimpled like turkey flesh. I knew how hurt she was.

I told her it had happened once, and that it had been in this room and on this bed, and as if it was the worst thing about the whole business she folded and unfolded her arms, put her hands in her pockets and drew them out, folded her arms again. She rubbed the skin around her elbows, crinkling it into circles. 'And you've never heard of decency? Did you have to do it? After all I've taught you?'

I felt as if I was in a room with a stranger from another country who wasn't using the right language.

'We didn't think.'

I watched how her hands fidgeted in the air, like birds with no resting place. I wanted to hold them still for her.

'It just happened.'

And Chris's photograph was a blur of colour on my table. I daren't look at it.

Mum gasped out again like a small child and came groping forward with her hands stretched out towards me, and I went up to her not knowing anything now, and she pressed me to her as if I was six years old.

'What are we going to do with you, child?' she whispered.

On Monday morning Mum took me to the doctor's. The waiting room was covered with posters saying, 'Don't let your baby nudge you into going to the doctor's.' I'd never noticed them before. I felt ashamed.

It wasn't my usual doctor. His examination was quick and professional. He told Mum I was probably twelve weeks' pregnant. My stomach plunged, even though I had known it for ages, for ever, it seemed. Everything felt as if it was draining out of me. To hear it said so clinically and finally was like being told 'Tomorrow you will hang' or something. I remember saying, 'I don't want a baby,' in a tiny weak voice that didn't sound like mine, and Mum sat there with her lips pursed tight while the doctor told us that if a termination was to take place it must be before sixteen weeks. 'Otherwise it will be very traumatic for you,' he said. My tears were as sharp as needles. I couldn't take in what he was saying. I have a baby inside me.

I've been in my room all day, writing this to you. I don't want to talk to anybody. I don't feel as if I have to, now. Mum will know what to do. The phone keeps ringing and it's always Mum who answers. I keep going to sleep and waking up, I'm not even sure if it's still the same day. The only thing I know for sure is that you're still there. It's growing dark, and I can hear the rain on the window, and it's comforting to hear it. I lay on my bed and let the darkness close in round me like a soft blanket. I could hear Robbie creeping upstairs to his room. He never creeps. He must have been told about me. And then I must have drifted off to sleep, because the click of the door woke me up, and there was Mum framed in the doorway with the full light behind her, and my room was in darkness. The light hurt my eyes. I was cold and stiff on top of my bed. Mum came over to me. I could hear her clothing rustling as she knelt down by me.

'You look like a little doll,' she said.

I turned away from her. Something was making my throat burn like fire.

Mum said, 'No one will know. Daddy won't know.'

I haven't called him Daddy since I was ten, I was thinking, and then she told me that the doctor had arranged everything, and that it would be all over by the end of the week, and as I listened to her whispering I felt as dry and bleached as a bone.

'You want to get it all over with quickly, don't you?' she said. I had to push the back of my hand into my mouth and bite it. The hurting in my throat had reached my eyes.

'You're not going to make a fuss, are you?'

I bit hard on the knuckles of my hand.

'Think of your future. It's your future. You mustn't throw it away,' and I shook my head, my eyes too full to see anything. My future is a deep, black well. Whatever I see in it frightens me. Mum touched my hair.

'You're only a child yourself,' she said.

She pulled my quilt up over me and I bit again on to my hand, all the aching in my throat and my neck and my shoulders swelling and tightening round me.

'And I've told Chris,' she said. 'You're not to get in touch with him. He agrees with me. It's for the best.'

I pretended I was asleep. I hadn't heard it. I could not put together the pieces of those words. When she went out of the room I could hear the swish of my green leotard on the door hook.

Dear Nobody. You did not ask for this. I have nothing to give you. Nothing. With all my heart I'm sorry.

★ ★ ★

When I rang Helen that night it was Mrs Garton who answered the phone.

'Just a minute,' she said.

I thought she'd gone to fetch Helen and I settled myself down on the bottom stair imagining her coming smiling to the phone, and then I heard a door being closed sharply, and the phone was picked up again.

'Hiya you,' I said.

'It's not Helen. She's asleep,' Mrs Garton said. I looked at my watch. It was eight o'clock. 'Listen,' she said, lowering her voice. It sounded as if she was hissing down the phone, but I think she was only trying to keep her voice down so nobody else could hear. But it made my skin creep, the way she hissed, and what she said to me. 'She's told me everything. I want you to know that you're never to come to this house again. Do you understand?'

I nodded, like a fool. Where were the words to answer her with? There aren't any. And her voice went on, a snake voice, a hissing dry and ice-cold sort of voice. 'She's decided to have an operation. Do you understand?'

I nodded again.

'It's the best thing, Chris. But you mustn't get in touch with her.'

I put the receiver down, with the words slithering round in my head. Guy went past with the washing he'd just taken from the dryer and headed a pair of rolled-up and still-warm socks at me, and when I didn't head them back he lobbed another pair at me from halfway up the stairs. I picked up the phone and rang again. As soon as Mrs Garton heard my voice she put the receiver down. I imagined her camped out for the night by the phone, her hand poised over the receiver. I desperately wanted to talk to Helen. I went up to my room with my legs feeling like lead weights, as if there was concrete in my shoes. The cat inched its way through the crack in the door and stared at me. It leapt on to my knee and I shook it off and it leapt up again. I reached over to my drawer and took out my file pad and balanced it on top of him. He rumbled as if I'd just switched him on.

Darling, darling Helen, I wrote.

Guy came in. I covered the paper with my hands.

'What're you doing?' he asked.

'Nothing,' I said. 'Get lost.'

'Who're you writing to?'

'Nobody. Clear off.'

'Can I take the cat?'

'No!' I yelled at him. 'For God's sake can't somebody even write a letter in peace!'

'I did your washing for you.' He ducked away as I screwed up the letter and hurled it at him. 'That's the last time I do your smelly underpants.' The cat sprang down on to the roll of paper and lay sideways with it stuck to one of the claws in his front paw, trying to knock it off with the other.

'Darling Nell,' I wrote. The letters swam round the page. 'It's my baby too. It's a little egg. It's life itself.' I didn't know what I was writing. To tell the truth I couldn't even see the page. 'Two hundred million sperm tried to reach you, and this is the one that made it. Nothing will ever be exactly like it again, ever, ever, in the world. It is unique. It is me in you, Helen, and you in me. Please don't destroy it. I love you, whatever you do.'

I couldn't read it afterwards. I felt blitzed, as if I'd been listening to crashing music and all of a sudden there was so much silence that I could drown in it. I put the letter in an envelope and sealed it.

I realized then that the house was in silence and that I'd been sitting holding the letter in my hand for hours, maybe. I went outside. The stars were out, kind of shivering. I wheeled my bike out of the yard and cruised down to Helen's on it. I tried throwing gravel up to her window but it showered back at me. I slid the letter through the letter box and waited with my fingers round it, expecting at any moment to feel it being taken away from me by another hand. I imagined her mother reading it, hating me for what I'd done to her daughter. Surely Helen would know I'd write to her if I couldn't reach her any other way. Surely she'd come down first thing and know there'd be a letter for her. I had to take the chance. I opened out my fingers, and listened to the soft flutter of the letter as it hit the floor.

I picked up my bike and carried it down the drive, trying to tiptoe on those red pebbles. The whole road echoed with the noise of my scrunching feet. And then I sat on the bike and looked back at the house and wondered whether I'd ever be welcome there again. For a crazy moment I thought of Helen's dad sneaking out to teach me some guitar chords, and for an even crazier moment I thought of shinning up the drainpipe to Helen's room and lying with her till dawn, like Romeo, till I was banished from the land, but I knew that I'd slide down it again like a fireman on a pole before I was a metre off the ground.

I didn't want to go home. I put my head down and bombed down the road at top speed, listening to the whirring of my wheels, and when I swung out on to the main road I headed off out to the moors. There were no cars on the road at all, nothing to hear, and when I left the street lamps behind and there was just the small light of my front lamp picking its way through the darkness and all that silence, it felt as if I was being eaten up by an enormous black mouth. I stood up on the pedals to make them turn faster; I don't know who I thought I was trying to race, or get away from; myself maybe, that little scared wretched self that had stood on Helen's doorstep.

It was uphill all the way, and I felt as if I was sweating inside a tight, hot glove, and then the road fell away and I freewheeled down to Fox House with the wind licking me. No houses or cars, no trees, only the dark clumps of heather and those looming cliffs. I knew exactly where I was going, and when the track got so bumpy that I was being flung about on my bike I hopped off it and left it leaning against a boulder. The moon was like a white face with a crooked smile, and I'm not kidding, those stars were like rocks. They were massive that night, white hanging rocks that could come crashing down from the sky at any minute. I jogged along till I was right under the Edge, and up above me, sixteen metres or so, was the little overhang that stuck out in front of Robin Hood's Cave.

I wanted to bring Helen here once. I wanted to spend the whole night with her, holding her and loving her, watching the sunset and then the stars and then the dawn.

I scrambled easily up the first bit, then had to search for handholds. The moon kept cutting out behind clouds. I heaved myself over the next bit and lay straddled across it, trying to get my breath back. I managed to stand up on a little ledge by inching myself up with my fingers, thinking all the time, thank God Tom isn't here, he'd have been up on to the top and down again by now, no problem, and then I made the mistake of looking down. I can't have been very far up but below me was blackness with little gleams of jagged edges, and I leaned against the cliff and very slowly it started to turn over, and over again, round and round like the Big Wheel at the fairground, swinging chairs and all, bloodbeats in your ears and your heart somewhere sliding round your tonsils; the whole mass of rocks and the whole starry space swinging up and round and over.

I don't know how I got back down. My skin had gone out of control like one of those freehand cartoon characters, but when I pulled myself together and looked up from solid ground I could see the ledge I'd been on, three metres off the ground – if that. I picked up a stone and hurled it against the ledge. The sound was like an explosion, ricocheting along the Edge. White boulders that were slumped under the Edge stood up and skittered away in fright, yelling to each other like sheep. I picked up another stone and flung it, and another and another, 'Bastard! Bastard! Bastard!' I roared, and my voice was a million miles away. 'B-A-S-T-A-R-D!'

It took me ages to find my bike. As soon as I started to ride it I hit a stone and the chain came off. It was jammed fast between the top gear and the frame, and I cut my thumb trying to jerk it out. I was swearing at the top of my voice all the time. I felt fantastic, in a loud, sweaty, oily, bloody, furious, sobbing sort of way.

And there was Sheffield, when the road tipped up to it at

last, a huge orange glow with millions of tiny winking lights set into it, and there was Helen's road, and the shops and the school. Our street and our house and the stairs. My room. And bed.

* * *

Dear Nobody,

It felt as if it was the last day of my life. Mum can't drive so I had to do it, and she never stopped talking. She kept reading out the street names as we passed them, and advertisements on hoardings, and even the registration numbers of the cars in front of us. It was as if she was frightened of silence. And all the time she was jabbering, I was forcing this into my head: this is simply an operation to remove unwanted cells from my body. That's all it is.

When I parked the car in the grounds of the hospital there was a dead bird on the grass verge, a tiny, skinny thing without feathers.

Mum sat with me while I was weighed and checked and then I had to change into a nightie. She put all my clothes into her bag. She was going to spend the night at her sister's, whose house was just down the road from the hospital. Aunty Pat would drive us back tomorrow. It was all carefully planned.

A doctor came in with a social worker and they sat and talked to me, and asked me if I was absolutely sure that this was what I wanted to do. My mouth didn't work properly. I wondered if they hated me. I wonder why they worked there. Then Mum held my hand and told me how brave I was being, and how I'd be able to go back to school at the end of the week and everything would be back to normal again. And then she couldn't bring herself to kiss me goodbye. I'd have put my arms around her if she had. I'd have asked her to stay with me because I was afraid.

The bed was high and the sheets were so stiff it was like lying between postcards. I lay on my side with my eyes closed and with my knees pulled right up to my chin and I tried to imagine what you looked like. You were twelve weeks old. You would be like a little pink tadpole. I'd looked you up in a medical book before we came. You would be about nine centimetres long. You weighed about fourteen grams.

I thought of myself on Nab's back, being thrown about like a doll, and I thought of you, a tiny thing, clinging on. You didn't think about anything and you didn't know anything and you clung on.

And when I was lying there, in all that silence, I felt as if it was me who was clinging on, as if you were my tiny self.

I felt as if you knew something that I would never understand. And I felt as if I had become two people.

I was still trying to focus on you, trying to see through my fear to what it was that I was really frightened of, when the nurse came in with a trolley. She came too soon. I wasn't ready yet. She didn't speak to me. She held a syringe up to the light, and I felt hot and scared. I was just on the edge of panic then. I asked her what it was for and she told me I was going to have my operation.

I wanted Chris.

I told her I needed to talk to someone, and she told me to hold myself still, that it wouldn't take a minute, that it wouldn't hurt, that it would all be over soon. I could hear her voice; I could hear mine in my head but I couldn't make the words come out. I was sobbing out loud. I was pushing her arm away. She said if I needed to talk to someone she'd better get someone. As soon as she was out of the room I felt as if I could breathe again. I slid out of my bed and put my slippers on. There was nothing in my locker except my little tapestry shoulder bag and my sponge bag and I picked them both up and went out. I thought at first that I was going to hide in the toilets but when I heard the nurse coming down the corridor talking to somebody I went straight past the toilets and found myself in the reception area. The receptionist had her back to me, looking for something in the filing cabinet and I walked straight past her and out through the doors into the car park. The keys were in my shoulder bag and my hands were shaking but I managed to get the car open and to drive it out into the road. I once saw a film that started in black and white and then went into full colour. All of a sudden I noticed that the leaves on the trees were full green. People had scarlet tulips blazing away in their front gardens. When I pulled up at the traffic lights the woman in the car next to me glanced across and then said something to her passenger, and they both looked at me then and laughed. I don't blame them for laughing. I chuckled back at them. I liked that nightie, but I would have liked to tell them that usually I sleep in a long tee shirt. No wonder I found it hard to drive; my slippers had bendy feet. I put a cassette on and wound down the windows and sang.

The worst bit came when I got home and had to walk over our pebbles in those bendy slippers.

I had a bath. I put a CD on really loud downstairs and left the bathroom door open. I hope you like music.

Then I got dressed in that lovely velvet skirt that I got from the fifties' shop and that I'm going to look terrible in soon, and drove to the library to find Dad. He was in the Local Studies section helping a student to find something.

I felt nervous when I saw him. I sat down and watched him, waiting for him to notice me. He had his hands clasped behind his back, and his fingers were moving one by one, as if he was practising piano scales. Maybe he was. He stoops a lot. He's so thin. He's such a quiet man.

The student said something that amused him and Dad put his hand up to his mouth and coughed gently, and then he saw me. He excused himself and came over, almost tiptoeing.

'What are you doing here?' he asked me.

I gave him the car keys.

'Mum's at Aunty Pat's,' I said. 'She'll be ringing you up soon. She wants you to drive her home.'

'I don't know what you mean,' he said. 'She said you'd both be at Pat's for a couple of days.'

All I wanted was for him just to take the car keys. But his face was full of questions. So I told him. 'I haven't been to Aunty Pat's at all,' I said. 'I'm going to have a baby.'

He looked so shocked and hurt that I took hold of his hand in both of mine. I told him about the abortion clinic. He tilted my head back and stared down at me as if he didn't recognize me; such a bewildered, anxious look. In a strange way I felt as if I was the one doing the consoling.

One of the library assistants came over and hovered just beside us, and when Dad noticed her he took his hand away from my chin and rested it on my shoulder. The librarian told him that his wife was on the phone. He followed her without looking back at me.

It was three o'clock when I left the library. I walked to Chris's school, taking a short cut through the park. It was full of young women with prams. I've never seen so many prams in my life before. The women all smiled at each other as they passed, as if there was some kind of conspiracy between them, as if they were members of a secret society.

Chris was one of the last to come out of the sixth-form block. He looked as if he'd been up all night. He was on his own, and he walked with his head down and his bag slung over his shoulder, as if he was miles away. He would have walked right past me if I hadn't called out to him. He went white when he saw me. I went up to him and waited for him to put his schoolbag down, and when his arms were round me, I told him.

Little Nobody. I won't let go of you now.

★ ★ ★

'What do we do now?'

It was all I could think of asking, and when Helen said, 'I don't know. You think of something,' I suggested that we should run off to our cave on the Derbyshire moors. It was meant as a joke, really, to make her smile again.

'That's just your trouble, Chris.' Her voice was tired and strained. She'd been through a hell of a lot that day. 'You're too romantic. We've got to be practical about this.'

'I've got twenty pounds,' I said. 'And a birthday coming up in August. I'll get a summer job.'

There was nothing going round here, and I knew it. Most of the people on my street hadn't got jobs at all, at any time of the year, let alone in the summer. I'd have to go down south to get anything, and then where would I live?

'And after that?' said Helen, in a quiet voice. 'When the baby's come? What do we do then, Chris?'

When I got home that night Dad and Guy were in the room, looking through a box of old photographs together. They were mostly of my gran and grandad, who'd both died before I was born. There were some of my dad when he was a little boy. I slumped in the cat's chair and watched them sorting through them. Dad was telling Guy the stories behind the photographs; we'd heard them lots of times before. I let their voices come and go; I was half-asleep, or half-drowning. Their voices were like pieces of driftwood keeping me afloat. 'I looked like you when I was your age, Chris,' Dad said. 'Just look at this one.'

I didn't want to look at anything. I didn't even want to open my eyes. Guy walked over to me on his knees and tugged my arm. I knew which photograph Dad was talking about even without looking. It was the one his father had taken of him in army uniform – short haircut, proud excited smile, off to do National Service. He did look like me. I used to look at it and think of him as a man. He wasn't. He was a boy with a fresh face and a shy smile.

'Was it in the war?' Guy asked.

'Was it heck!' said Dad. 'I'm not that old. Besides, I wouldn't have been grinning my socks off if I thought I was setting off to get blown to pieces, would I?'

He leaned across and took the photograph back, and looked at it curiously, wiping the surface with the tip of his finger as if he was trying to touch that boy's face from the past.

'Don't know myself!' he laughed. 'It feels like another lifetime. Thought the whole world was mine, in those days. Just like you do, Chris.'

I closed my eyes.

'Only your chances are better than mine ever were,' Dad went on. Helpless, I floated away from his voice. 'Make the most of them. You can never start again.'

Dear Nobody,

When she came home from Aunty Pat's my mother, your grandmother, walked past me as if she didn't know me. I was sitting in the kitchen waiting for her to come and when I heard the car I went to open the door. I'd made myself look nice for her and I'd started the tea. She walked past me and went upstairs, and on her way up she said, without looking at me, 'You've let me down, Helen.'

I had to let somebody down.

Dad came in behind her with his car keys dangling in his fingers. He gave me a worried look and made to go into his piano room, to lock himself away in there and lose himself in his music. That's his escape – that's my escape too, but not this time. I followed him in and sat on the piano stool before he could get to it, and turned to face him.

'What did she say?' I asked him.

'She's very upset, Helen.'

'Of course she's upset,' I told him. 'But will she let me stay here?'

He looked alarmed. 'Good God, she's not going to kick you out into the streets.'

'But will she let me live here, with a baby?'

'You're not really going to keep it, love?' His voice was pleading.

I knew I was going to break down again, and I thought, is the crying never going to stop, is there no end to all this? I could feel my breath coming in little gasps. It was better not to speak after all. I turned my back on him and raised the piano lid. It was what he'd have done, and I couldn't help it; it was inside me, just as you are, just as much a part of me as my blood and my breath. I began to play; I don't know what it was, I was making it up as I went along and I heard him talking to me still, under the rolling ocean of my music.

'I'd have given anything in the world to go to music school. Do you know that?'

I'd never heard him raise his voice in anger before – or was it grief?

I didn't want to hear him. I let the dark chords roll.

'You're throwing your life away.'

May

Helen and I tried to spend all our time together after that. I think that week or so after the clinic were the best we ever had together. It was as if we were one person, bound up in each other's present. The future and the past were outer space.

'What will we do, though?' Helen would ask me from time to time, or I would ask her, and the answer was always that we didn't know; space was too vast for us to enter yet.

'But we'll be together, whatever happens.'

I was never allowed to go round to her house, or to try to phone her up. I wanted more and more time with her. That was why, when I met her brother Robbie one afternoon on his way home from school, I bribed him to take her a message. He looked cautious. He'd obviously been well primed by Alice Garton.

'I'll give you a Mars bar,' I offered, and when he began

to soften, 'It's a really important secret mission, Robbie, and you're the only person who can do it.'

I wanted her to meet me at the railway station on May 15th at eight o'clock. I could hardly believe it when I saw her there. She was standing by the bookstall reading a Thomas Hardy novel.

'Are you nervous?' she asked me, as our train arrived.

'As hell,' I said.

'It'll be all right,' she said.

The train was crowded and noisy. We were glad to get off at Manchester and change trains.

'How d'you feel about it?' I asked her.

'Okay,' she smiled.

We stood on the platform holding hands and staring in front of us, each of us locked into our own thoughts.

When our train came we held hands all the way to Carlisle. She wasn't showing yet. You wouldn't have thought there was anything different about her at all, but we knew. It was a secret between us that made us squeeze each other's hand from time to time without looking at each other. There's something very private and special about that, holding hands, and not looking at each other, and knowing just how full and warm the other one is feeling. When I first saw Helen I liked her because she looked friendly and calm, there's a kind of steadiness about her that tells you she won't go off into sulks or anything. I can't say I like girls who sulk. But after a bit I knew that the thing I liked most about her was her smile. She's quite a serious person really, a bit like her dad, and when you're talking to her she studies you quietly as if she's trying to read your mind, and that's a bit unnerving. It makes you crack daft jokes to try to distract her, in a way. And then all of a sudden she'll smile, and that just transforms her. She really is stunning when she smiles. And for weeks she wasn't smiling any more and her eyes had gone strained and scared, and she looked ill. It was awful, that. I knew I'd done that to her, and that I'd taken that terrific smile away. And now she was well and happy again, and when I squeezed her hand I knew she was smiling, even though she was gazing out of a train window and I was reading a book, and I was warm and dizzy, knowing it. I couldn't help holding her hand. I wanted to touch her all the time.

She doesn't talk about what it's like at home. I had been forbidden to go there any more, of course. I think her mother wished me dead, quite honestly.

Her mother and father came round to see my dad, soon after that do at the clinic. I wasn't in. Thank goodness I wasn't in. I was refereeing a football match in the rain, wishing I wasn't at the time, and when I came home they'd gone. They didn't stay long, apparently. Alice Garton had prepared what she wanted to say and she said it without stopping. She was very angry, I heard. Mr Garton just kept clearing his throat and taking his glasses off and polishing them on his tie. My dad just sat and listened. When I came home he was still sitting there. The television was switched on without any sound. It was a crazy, flickering thing in the corner of the room, and Dad was sitting staring at it with a kind of cold and heavy silence round him, as if he was wrapped up in a winter coat that still had bits of snowflakes clinging to it. I could tell the Gartons had been. I almost went straight up to my room but Dad just raised his hand slightly and I sat down on the edge of the cat's armchair.

'I wish you'd told me,' he said. 'That woman comes here, shouting her mouth off. Says you've got to marry Helen. I don't know what the hell's going on, do I?'

'I wanted to tell you.' I couldn't get the frog out of my throat. I imagined it squatting under my tonsils, its bright eyes blinking down my windpipe.

'The thing about lads,' Dad said, 'is that they can get away scot-free if they want to. Or they think they can.'

The television screen flashed away like a dumb caged beast desperate to escape.

I cleared my throat. 'I don't want to.'

'So what are you planning to do about it? Are you telling me you two want to get wed, at the age of eighteen?'

Marriage, and a flat somewhere. A mortgage stretching into middle age, till I was older than my dad. The idea scared the wits out of me. Think about re-incarnation. Get it right next time round.

'What do you want then? What about your degree? What about Newcastle?'

I closed my eyes. I wished he'd stop.

'You're not expecting to take her with you, are you? Away from her family and her pals? What would she do, that lass, stuck in a student's bedsit in the middle of Newcastle? Stuck in with a baby?'

That frog had crawled up my windpipe again.

'She's reckoned to be a very clever lass, that Helen.'

'She is,' I muttered. 'She's brilliant.'

'Are you expecting her to throw up all her chances too? What the hell were you thinking of?'

Everything was blurring. The lights from the television were sharp and dazzling.

'Her mother says either you marry the girl or you're not to see her again. I can't say I blame her. Mind you, what's done is done.'

I put out my hand to stroke the cat, for its warmth and comfort, and very neatly and tenderly it placed its teeth round my finger. As long as I didn't pull my hand away it wouldn't bite. I prised my finger free and stood up, and Dad stood up too. He flicked off the TV and came over to me. He has that slight limp, Dad, only very slight, from an accident at work. When I was little some of my friends were scared to come in the house. He just came over to me, shaking his head a little, and because I was scared then I went to walk away, and, as if he couldn't help it, he put his arm across my shoulder. 'Don't think I'm not sorry for you,' he said.

I wanted Mum, then, too.

* * *

May 15th

Dear Nobody,

I must have been mad, going all that way with Chris. I did it because it was a way of spending some time with him. I pretended to Mum that it was a school trip, even though I haven't been into school for ages. It's awful to tell lies to your own mother. I hated doing it. But she's not the sort of mother that you can tell the truth to, most of the time. She doesn't want to hear it. She doesn't want to hear about you, little Nobody. You don't exist. We don't talk about you.

And because we don't talk about you we don't talk about anything. I've lost my mum. We walk past each other like strangers in the house. I eat in my own room because I can't find anything to say, because I can't bear the atmosphere downstairs, because I'm an outcast in my own family. Dad treats me as if I was made of glass, asks me if I'm feeling well, puts cushions behind me when I'm sitting down. But he doesn't lean over the piano when I'm playing and jazz up Chopin with his left hand, and he doesn't tease me about Chris, or play his old ragtime records and tap-dance in the kitchen, self-mocking, happy.

It's my fault, all this.

So when Chris asked me to go to Carlisle with him to meet his mother I said yes. In a frantic sort of way, I felt it would bring me in touch with my own mother again.

He was a bag of nerves by the time we found her road. I think he would have preferred to turn round and catch the next train home. 'Anyone would think you were about to have your boils lanced,' I told him. But I knew exactly how he felt. Little Nobody, don't ever be a stranger to me.

Chris's mother smokes, so that gave her minus points from the start. I could smell it on her breath when she came to answer the door, and on her clothes. They stank, actually. She was really pretty and she stank. In a way it gave me courage about meeting her, because I knew then that she couldn't tell us off or try to dictate to us what we ought to do. No one who pumps nicotine into themselves or fouls up the air for other people has the right to tell anyone what to do with their lives, that's what I think. So I felt confident, as soon as I smelt her. No one's going to breathe that lousy muck over you. I won't let them.

She looks years younger than Chris's dad. She didn't wear make-up or tidy clothes or anything like that but she looked really pretty, with her hair cropped short like a boy's and her enormous dark eyes. Actually, Chris has her eyes. She looked happy, too. I suppose it's climbing that does it, all that fresh air and exercise. It's a pity about the smoking. I actually think I might have liked her except for that. I could tell Chris was really excited to be with her; he kept grinning and running his hands through his hair. I wanted to smooth it down again for him when it went spiky in the middle. I wonder if she wanted to, as well.

Her new bloke was there, too. He just looked like all the climbers I've ever seen on Stanage Edge, he even had the greying beard. I've seen them clinking along with ropes slung round their shoulders and all kinds of hooks and crampon things jingling off them.

It was really hot that day, and he was wearing shorts. His legs are very hairy. I wouldn't mind betting that he's hairy all over, actually. He had a little knot of varicose veins like a tiny bunch of grapes just below his knee. I noticed them when he sat down. When he saw me looking at them he dangled his hand over them.

I wandered round the house because I felt too edgy to settle. She kept calling Chris Christopher and telling him that he was tall, as if he didn't know, and she asked him about Guy and school and she even remembered the cat. She never mentioned his dad, I noticed. I wonder what happened. It was easier to imagine them apart than together, but they must have been in love at one time. It's strange to think that people can fall in love and out of it again, that love can turn to hate, and that it's the people who loved you most who could hurt you most. I know that because people have told me that, and because I've read it in novels, but I don't understand it. I don't understand what it is that makes my mum and dad into a couple, for instance. He's only happy reading, or playing the piano. I can't imagine them kissing, or holding hands, or whispering to each other. I suppose they must have done, once. But then, I don't understand what love is, either. I don't understand how it can take over, overwhelm you like a huge breaker, knocking the breath out of you, swamping you. I thought of all the lads in Yorkshire, say, thousands of them, and I could have met and liked any one of them, perhaps, but it was Chris who took over. How can it be that there's not a moment of any day when I'm not thinking about him, and yet I seemed to have plenty of things to think about before. I sometimes feel as if I'm not flesh and blood and bone but I'm made up of millions and millions of minute pieces of mirror-glass, and one side of every piece reflects me, and the other reflects Chris, and they're spinning and spinning, like the dust in the sunlight, and yet I'm walking about and nobody notices anything different about me.

All the while she was talking to Chris I felt as if I was squatting inside his head listening to her, and feeling tense and uncomfortable and happy for him, all at the same time. I wandered round, looking at her photographs. She had them all over the walls. She gave me one because I took it down and asked her about it. It was a long kind of spiny ridge of mountain, and it sloped down to a lake. She said it was Catbells, above Derwent Water in the Lake District. It had a wonderful, calm atmosphere about it, and it was almost a double image because the whole thing was reflected in the lake, mountains upside down, sky turned to water. It was nice of her to give it to me. I want to go there, but I'll wait till you can come too. That's daft, isn't it? I mean, you come everywhere now. One day I'll take you in a rowing boat right out to the middle of the lake, and you'll look up at all the ridges and fells around you.

'These are for you, little Nobody,' I'll say. 'I'm giving you the world.'

I can't even think what's going to happen next. But that photograph is like a bridge, somehow, taking me over to the other side of a black chasm of nothingness.

On the journey up, Chris had said that he wasn't going all that way just to say how nice the lentil soup was and to tell her where he was going for his holidays. He said he wanted to tell her about the most important things in his life, and we both curled up when he said that, you and I, we both felt warm and safe for a bit. I laugh at Chris sometimes when he's like that, and I get impatient about it and tell him off for being romantic and I get embarrassed, too, in case anyone else can see the way he looks at me. But I'm glad.

And it *was* lentil soup. I couldn't look at Chris when she brought it in. It was lovely, though, brown lentils with onions, and lots of thick bread with bits in it. And when she said, 'Have either of you made any holiday plans yet?' just to make conversation, and Chris smiled and hesitated for one second, I came straight out with it. 'I don't think I'll be going anywhere,' I said. 'I'm having a baby in the autumn.'

I wish I'd waited till we'd finished the soup.

'Oh, I see,' she said, and she kept looking from one to the other of us as if she was trying to catch us out. Some people have their feelings written all over their faces. I had no idea what she was thinking. Her bloke had just put a spoonful of soup into his mouth and he choked on it. We all sat in total silence with lentil soup dripping off our spoons and him making little spurting noises at the back of his throat because he was trying not to cough out loud. His face was going scarlet and his eyes were watering, and he was swallowing in tiny, fast gulps with his mouth shut tight and his Adam's apple poking up and down over the hairs at the neck of his tee shirt.

'For God's sake get a drink of water, Don,' she snapped, and he jumped up and ran into the kitchen with his hand over his mouth and soup dribbling down his chin. He coughed out loud as soon as he was out of sight, more like barking really, and he didn't come back to the table again. He was probably embarrassed because he thought he'd made a fool of himself, after all that posing about he'd done with his hairy legs. I once went out with a bloke before I met Chris. He was older than me, and I was impressed because he was a systems analyst. He took me out for a meal at a restaurant. I thought we were just going in for a coffee and I didn't like to tell him that I'd already had my tea. He ordered fresh salmon for us both. I'd never had fresh salmon before, and I didn't know about the bones. With tinned salmon they're just little scrunchy things, a bit like chunks of Edinburgh rock. So I put a forkful into my mouth and then found it was full of bones that I couldn't bite or chew or swallow, and I didn't know what on earth to do, and this bloke kept looking at me and talking to me really earnestly about computer programs all the time, so I couldn't spit them out. My eyes were streaming, just like her hairy husband's. In the end I just stood up and went to the ladies and got rid of them. I stood there for ages, daring myself to go back in and face the rest of the bones, and then I opened the wrong door and found I wasn't back in the restaurant but out in the street. So I caught a bus home. I suppose it was an awful thing to do, and I hope I never bump into him again. I suppose I could offer to pay for the meal. But he was very boring. And he hadn't even asked me whether I wanted salmon.

I sat at the table grinning about it and started tucking into my lentil soup before it went cold, and Chris's mother leaned forward and began to drill me with questions, how old was I and was I sure and what arrangements had I made, and in the end I felt like crying and I blurted out, 'It's Chris's baby too!' She laughed out loud, a cold sharp laugh, and fished her cigarettes out of her pocket. I can't stand people who smoke when you're eating. It's all you can taste. So I asked if I could have some more lentil soup because it really was lovely, and then I wandered outside with it and sat on a bench in her garden to eat it. I stopped boiling up inside after a bit. I felt warm and sleepy in the sun. I could hear her and Chris talking, and their voices were coming in and out like waves because I was nearly asleep, and then I heard him telling her that he wasn't going to give up his degree.

I went into the kitchen and made a lot of noise washing up my soup bowl and dropping spoons on the floor and looking for something else to eat. I was famished. Fancy letting people come all that way and not cooking a proper meal for them. Not even people. Your own son, for goodness' sake. I could have wept for Chris, I was so disappointed for him. I looked in the fridge and saw four plates of cheese salad and took one of them outside. Chris and his mum were still talking by the time I'd eaten it so I took two of the other plates and put them on the table in front of them. Chris would be starving. We'd left home at six. I pretended I was a waitress in a café, discreet and dumb, and Chris glanced up and put his hand over mine and squeezed it.

'I'll be in the garden,' I said.

I helped myself to a yoghurt and wandered out again. She followed me out a bit later. Chris was washing up in the kitchen. She looked a bit surprised to see me eating a yoghurt and I realized that they probably hadn't been meant for pudding after all. I finished it, anyway. Yoghurts don't cost much.

She sat on the grass watching me, pursing her lips now and again to blow out smoke. Her fingers were tap-tap-tapping ash on to the lawn. She looked composed and at ease with herself, but I've got a feeling she was nervous and at a bit of a loss. It must have been a strain for her, seeing Chris again after all those years. I bet she was knotted up inside, in spite of looking so calm and easy. I bet she went to bed with a headache as soon as we'd gone. I wonder if she usually smoked as much as that. I coughed and she moved her hand away so the smoke spiralled up behind her.

'Christopher tells me you're in the sixth form, too, Helen,' she said. She has a nice voice. Posher than Chris's or his dad's. I think she must have married beneath her, as my mum would say. Isn't that daft? How can someone be less than somebody else just because they say their words in a different way or they come from a different part of town? What if they were brilliant at playing the flute or dressmaking or growing tomatoes or building cupboards?

I thought of Chris's dad, bending over his potting wheel, his breath thick and thoughtful and satisfied, and his big hands shaping those lovely jugs and pots he makes. I'd rather have him than Hairy-legs, any day.

I told her that I didn't go to Chris's school because they didn't offer music in the sixth form.

'Music?' she raised her eyebrows. I'd been through her pile of CDs. She's really into Mozart. 'That's nice. What else are you doing?'

I told her, General, because everyone has a go at that, and Maths, Latin and Dance, and she raised her eyebrows again and I went quiet. It isn't your fault, little Nobody. I don't think about Dance any more. I've put my leotard away in a drawer. It's better if I don't see it again, that's all.

'Music, Latin, Maths and Dance,' she murmured, as if it was a line from a poem. 'You like patterns, then.'

I thought that was a really good thing to say. I love it when people think sideways.

'And your exams start next month?'

I thought she hadn't understood me, then. I thought she'd forgotten about you. Nothing's happening between now and you. It's a void. A tunnel. When I think about it I slide down into it myself. I turn myself inside out and find myself in the dark tunnel with you.

'I hope you do well, Helen,' she said. Her smile was so warm and encouraging that it made me like her again. 'You owe it to yourself, and to your mum and dad.' She leaned forward and patted my stomach, and it was such an odd and intimate and cheeky thing to do that I laughed out loud with surprise, and so did she. 'And you owe it to this little thing.'

Did you feel that, Nobody? Did you hear it? That was your grandmother talking. Bet she doesn't like that, the idea of being a grandmother. Funny how grandmothers in stories are white-haired and whiskery and keep losing their hearing aids, and yours is slim and pretty and is a well-known climber.

Chris and I were very quiet, going home on the train. He put his arm round me and I snuggled up with my head lolling under his shoulder. I think he thought I was asleep. But I wasn't. I was plotting my revision timetable. I'd ring Ruthlyn tomorrow and get her to come round and go through some maths with me. I was okay with Music and Latin. Can't revise for General. Dance. Well, Dance would depend on how I feel. But I feel fantastic. I'll talk to Doctor Phillips about it, and see what she says. It's not too late. I've already got my full offer at the music college. One day I might go there still. I could feel a kind of excitement bubbling up in me. It's not too late. I said it over and over again in time to the train. Tantivy tantivy tantivy. There's time there's time there's time.

We'll do it together, little Nobody.

★ ★ ★

It was the weirdest experience, meeting my mother again, seeing her not as a ghost or an ogre or as some wonderful enchanted being but as a woman. She was prettier than I expected her to be. I don't know why this surprised me; maybe it's because my dad is such an ordinary-looking bloke. And she was very nervous, too. The air was electric. I think Helen was the only calm one among us when we first arrived, and she kept prowling round the room like a lion in a cage, noseying through my mother's books and CD collection, taking down the photographs from the walls. The meal was really uncomfortable. It's bad enough eating in front of strangers at the best of times, but when that stranger is your own mother it's a kind of torture. It gives you something to do with your hands, I suppose, but it blocks up your mouth.

I could tell Don didn't want to be with us at all. It must have been worse for him than for any of us. I thought he was very sensitive, the way he sat back and let my mother do the talking, not trying to butt in or ask questions – just supporting her, I suppose. Then Helen blasted them with a bombshell and the poor bloke couldn't take it. He used it as an excuse to get out of the house altogether, and it must have been a relief for him. It was certainly a relief for me. And then it all seemed to be a bit much for Helen and she wandered out into the garden. So we were alone together, my mother and I. That was when the talking really began.

'I admire you for coming,' she said. 'It was brave of you. You're braver than me.'

'I've been wanting to see you for ages,' I said. 'Before, you know, before Helen was . . . you know.'

'I think of you as a little boy of ten with a passion for model trains and Batman, with a little high voice and a freckly face, and I meet a young man who is in love and who is fathering a child.'

Even without the lentil soup I found swallowing hard.

'What will you do?' she asked.

'I don't know,' I said.

'What do you want to do?'

'Everything.' I kept trying to swallow. 'I want to do my degree at Newcastle.' I looked down at my hands. 'And I want to be with Helen. I don't really know what she wants. She doesn't know.'

'Christopher,' she said, 'I did a terrible thing when I left your father.'

'I know.'

'But before that I had done an even worse thing, and that was to marry him in the first place.'

My eyes were smarting. I couldn't look at her then.

'Can I tell you about it?'

'If you want to.' I didn't know whether I wanted to know or not. Was this what I'd come for? I'd no idea.

'I was probably younger than Helen when I met Alan. My dad died when I was twelve. My mum couldn't cope after that. Sometimes things like that give people a strength they didn't know they had; sometimes it takes all their strength away from them. I was brought up by my grandmother, and she loved my sister best. But then, everyone loves Jill best. I left school at sixteen, though I was clever enough to do other things, they reckoned. I'd had enough, you know. I needed to be myself by then, prove myself – you understand that. We do the wrong things for the right reasons sometimes. I met your father at work. He was one of the labourers and I was an office girl. He used to come and sit by me in the yard at lunch break and talk to me. Do you know, I think he reminded me of my dad? I think I thought I loved him, and all the time it was because he was bringing my dad back to me.

He was ten years older than me, and very quiet and sensitive. He thought the world of me; he adored me. He made me feel special again, and wanted. And he had a house. He begged me to marry him. It was my escape. And I thought I loved him. Maybe I did, but it wasn't the right kind of love.'

Helen was rooting round in the kitchen, dropping spoons and things. I thought of Dad, my gentle, kind, thoughtful dad, and I wanted to cry for him, I really did. My mother and I sat without talking for ages and Helen came in, trying to be discreet, tiptoeing round us with plates of salad. It was as if she had drawn back the curtains to let in the sunlight. I felt myself relaxing. I put my hand on hers just to let her know something.

'I'll be in the garden,' she said.

The house was quiet again.

'And then you met Don.'

'I met Don. It was a couple of years after Guy was born. I started to join clubs and things, you know, just to get out. Your dad loved you kids. He'd do anything for you. The only thing he wanted at night was to stay in with you, read to you, play Subbuteo and build Lego things. I needed to get out. He didn't mind. I joined a climbing club and that's where it all started. I fell in love, really fell in love. I was twenty-six and I had two children and for the first time in my life I was in love. Too late. Much too late. I couldn't stand it. I didn't know what to do with myself. I thought I was dying, Christopher, and that's the truth. I thought the real me was dying. I don't excuse myself and I don't forgive myself but there was only one thing I could do to keep my real self alive and that was to go with Don, and after nearly four years of worrying about it I did it.'

She shoved her plate away and fished in her pockets for her cigarettes and then shoved them away too.

'I started smoking these damn things again when you sent me that first letter.'

'You didn't want to see me.'

'I couldn't bear to see you, not when you were little. I felt terrible about leaving Alan. I was in love with Don and I'd got what I wanted and we were together, and I'd left behind my two children to do it. I grieved for you boys. Every day for months I was on the point of coming back, and if I had done it would have been to say goodbye to the real me for ever. What I wanted most was to be with Don and to have you with me, too. But I loved Alan, not as a wife should, but as a daughter, maybe, as a friend. I couldn't take his children away from him as well. How could I have done that to him? I made a decision never to get in touch with you boys again. I suppose I was punishing myself. I know now that it was the wrong decision.'

Hours later, when I was on the train, her words were still going round and round in my head, like tiny mice running through a network of tunnels, into air and into darkness, out into air again, running and running. Helen was asleep I think, snuggled up under my shoulder. I was glad. I didn't want to have to talk.

June

I couldn't believe how cold it was, the morning of the first English paper. People had always told me that there would be a heatwave in June, it's traditional, right up till the end of the exams. They said I'd get hayfever and spend the exams sniffling and not being able to read the question paper properly because my eyes were running, and that the sun would be scorching the back of my neck while I was sweating over the questions. But it wasn't like that this year. My feet were freezing in the school hall. I wished I'd put my hiking socks on. I'd been awake all night anyway chasing quotes from *Hamlet* and *Much Ado* round my head. I'd got Sociology that afternoon and my head was full of names and dates and theories about that, too. I was banking on Gender and Education coming up.

I couldn't help thinking what a waste of time it all was. Really. Not the learning; the revising. Like eating a massive meal when you only want a sandwich. Then you puke it all up for the examiners and stuff yourself up again for the next day.

They reckon you can get high on revising, like people on speed. You get into a state of unreality, where what's going on in your head is more meaningful than what's going on in the real world. Anyway, what is the real world? Maybe the only reality is what you happen to be thinking or experiencing at any given time.

While I was revising for the first English paper *Hamlet* was going on in my head all the time, like another life I was leading at the same time as my own life. He could have come into our kitchen at any time in his doublet and hose and I wouldn't have been at all surprised. 'Now then, Hamlet,' I'd have said, mashing him a cup of tea, 'let's talk about your mum.' And maybe he'd have said, 'Good Kit, 'tis in our hearts to speak of mothers now, but what of sweethearts, tell me that?' Or something like that, except he'd get the iambic pentameter right, and Ophelia would have come in, white and dripping all over the floor and carrying flowers, holding Helen's hand.

I'm going mad. Foolish prating knave.

Do I want to do an English degree anyway? What's it all for? I want Helen.

She rang me up to wish me luck before I left home. I could tell by the sound of the traffic that she was using the phone at the top of her road. Her first exam would be the next day. Music. She'll waltz through it. She'd waltz through any exam she took. I don't think I've ever met anyone as clever as Helen.

I felt all right till I actually got to the school hall, and then when I saw everyone fidgeting outside, all dropping their pens and their rulers and saying that they hadn't done a stroke, I started to panic. The place was humming with tension, as if the room was strung up with pylon wires. Tom was striding up and down gabbling reams of quotes as if they were shopping lists, all in a jumble, and saying, 'What play's that from? Who's the old guy who gets stabbed?' and 'Is *Hamlet* the play with the balcony scene?'

'You're making me as nervous as hell,' I told him.

He stuck his hand out for me to shake. 'Good luck, comrade,' he said. 'If it were done when 'tis done, then t'were well it were done quickly.'

'Get lost,' I said.

I took a deep breath then before I went in, as if I was about to launch myself off the high-dive. I didn't even know what I was going to do in October. It was all a confusion. I didn't know what I wanted, today, tomorrow, next year, ever. I didn't know what Helen wanted. We hadn't even talked about it. Somehow, we couldn't – it's too dangerous to put all that into words; searchlights probing into darkness, picking out creeping, scared soldiers. Gunning them down forever. My dad was insisting that we made some plans, and the more he insisted the more I resisted. 'The problem won't go away, you know,' he said to me. 'It'll get worse. The longer you leave it, the worse it will get.' When he gets a bill he can't pay he hides it behind the clock for a bit. I could have reminded him about this, but I didn't. Helen and I told each other we'd talk properly after the exams, get them out of the way. It's all too much to carry, all at once.

Helen should be taking her place at the Royal Northern College of Music in October. I should be taking mine at Newcastle University. That was how our future looked six months ago, anyway. It had looked like two separate pictures; now they were both shattered and shuffled up together, like collapsed houses of cards.

Our Head of English, Hippy Harrington, grinned at me as I went into the hall and gave me a discreet wink. I walked down the rows of desks, looking for M for Marshall, and all of a sudden I felt calm. Helen was well and happy, after that terrible start. Did anything else matter? Soon, irrevocably, there would be a baby that was hers and mine, she and me. Nothing was going to stop that happening. If she could feel calm about these things, then so could I. I sat down and laid out my pens in a neat row. When the signal was given I turned over the paper. There was the first context question. 'What! my Lady Disdain . . .' I could imagine Helen, pursing her lips, tilting back her head at me. My dear Lady Nell. Soon we'll know what to do.

★ ★ ★

June 6th

Dear Nobody,

Today two things happened to me.

You moved. Deep inside me I felt a fluttering, and I knew that you had moved. You arched your back or something, turned over in your sleep, I don't know – unsucked your thumb, maybe, whatever it was, I felt it. It was like a tiny bird fluttering. You are arms and legs and fingers, you are moving parts. You are a little amazing piece of machinery.

Soon you won't be a secret any more. Already my waist has disappeared and my stomach is rounding out. Just slightly. I can hide it, you, with loose shirts. But soon the women in the park will know me for what I am. I'll be one of them, part of their conspiracy, and we'll smile at one another knowingly.

It's like winter today. I'm cold to the bone. Are you warm enough, tucked up in there?

Listen.

Can you hear the rain?

I'm glad the exams have started. I wish Mum would relax about Chris. It would be wonderful to be revising together, to have him here at home and spend time together, listen to music and drink coffee when we want a break, walk out for air with rain on our faces. But she won't hear of it. He's not allowed here, ever again. She won't even talk to me about him, or you.

Sometimes Dad comes and sits with me on the settee or in the piano room and he'll say something like: 'Your mother wants to know what your plans are, Helen.' But she won't bring herself to ask me herself, and that's what hurts most.

I always say, 'Don't ask me, Dad. I don't know yet.'

Sometimes he just squeezes my hand, and I feel like crying then. I want to put my head on his shoulder and cry and cry, but I don't think he'd know how to cope with that. So I hold it back, and he gives me the little prepared speech that she's told him to say, about wasting my life.

'What do you want me to do, Dad?' I asked him yesterday. I knew the answer.

'I want you to do Music.'

That's it. It's so simple for him. He's not facing the facts any more than she is, so how can they blame me?

Anyway, I *have* come to a decision, and that was the other thing that happened to me today. I've decided that I must finish with Chris.

You see, I know I'm ready for you. I know I can cope. I was afraid of you once. Now, every inch of me wants you, and I'll bide my time and when we're ready I'll go to Music College and you'll share my future with me. You're all I can think about. I'm turned inside out, like a bud with all its perfume and colour locked inside it. Every second of the day I'm aware of you.

But I'm not ready for Chris.

I'm not ready to share my life with him, and that's what it would mean. The thought of it terrifies me. He's all keyed up for Newcastle, and university life. He's talked of nothing else since I met him. I know he'd stay with me if I asked him to. It would be asking him to make an enormous sacrifice but I'm pretty sure he'd do it. I know we'd find a flat somewhere and maybe his dad and my dad would help us out. I'd lose my mum forever. But we'd do our best to make things right for you.

Yet I hurt inside when I think about it. I wake up in terror, Nobody, and I don't know what it is I'm more frightened of: promising myself to Chris forever, or spending forever without him. I don't know him yet. Six months ago the thought of spending the rest of our lives together had never entered our heads. We were a pair of kids having fun together. And now we've been catapulted into the world of grown-ups. I'm not ready for forever. I'm not ready for him, and he's not ready for me. And more than anything else, I'm afraid of all this hurt touching you. Does it? Can you tell?

I'm going to wait till his exams finish before I tell him. It would be cruel to do it now, but I mustn't just let it slide, just wait till you're born, just let things happen as if nothing could be helped or stopped or thought about. Chris and I will have a lovely last few weeks together – I'll see him every day if I can.

And then, when the exams are over, I'll tell him.

June 15th

Dear Nobody,

I walked with Robbie to Grandad's this morning. If Grandad doesn't know already, I've decided, I must tell him about you. Mum won't have told him, that's for sure. They're so secretive, my family.

It's cold. June should be sunshine and strawberries, cotton dresses, bees in roses, but it's all grey skies and cold winds. The weather's closed in round us, like concrete walls. We've got the central heating on at home, and last night Mum took a hot-water bottle to bed. It feels more like winter, she said.

My exams have finished now. I just put my head down and got on with them. I actually enjoyed them. I think I was high on adrenalin, actually, after all that revising and all that agonizing about Chris. I poured myself into them, and felt myself soaring through them.

Success is like a bright star that you hold out both hands for. I do want to succeed, little Nobody. Now, for both our sakes, I want to shine.

Before the exams started I met Ruthlyn and the other girls in the school foyer. I felt as if it was a hundred years since I'd seen any of them, except Ruthlyn. Ruthlyn was fine with me, of course. Good old Ruthlyn. She knows now. She said she's always known, but she just waited for me to tell her. I wish she wasn't going away. It would be a lot of fun, sharing a flat with Ruthlyn. She'd be brilliant at helping with you. Just while we were waiting to go in to the first exam she started to tell me a story about when her sister Grace was pregnant and had such a craving for coal that she used to crunch lumps of it as if they were sweets. She was trying to whisper but she's got such a loud voice you could hear her over a rock band. I suppose we were a bit tense as well, I mean it was the Applied Maths exam we were going into, but she got me really giggling. I could tell all the other girls were hating us. They're real bores, some of these maths girls. They wear triangle skirts and white socks. Funny, lots of the music students are like that too. I used to like them, actually. Now I don't know what to say to them. I feel like a curiosity, the way they all glance at my stomach and look away again, the way they turn to each other and smile. But I want to say, 'I'm still the same person, you know. I haven't changed.'

But I'm not the same person, and I never will be, ever again.

They're shy of me, I suppose, and so is Chris, in a strange way. I couldn't wait to tell him that I'd felt you moving inside me and he looked at me in a grinning, embarrassed sort of way. 'Put your hands on my tummy,' I told him. 'You might feel it, too.' But he wouldn't.

If he's shy of you, and of me, how can he ever be a father to you? I know I'm right. We don't touch now, not in that intimate way. We don't stroke each other. We hold hands and kiss, and I yearn for him, but I'm scared. Now that it's too late, I'm scared. What would we be doing, if we lived together and we were afraid to touch each other? He's got his English Paper Three to take, and then I'll tell him.

So, anyway, I went to Grandad's with Robbie. Robbie is such a pain these days. His teeth keep growing. I'm sure they do. I'm sure his teeth weren't that big this time last year. All ten-year-old boys seem to have huge front teeth. I can't understand it. And he's always giggling about things. He used to be a little boy that I could tell stories to and play rounders with. Not long ago.

On the way to Grandad's he said, 'When are you going to – you know what?' and he started giggling in this silly high-pitched baby giggle voice of his, and little watery bubbles kept fluffing out between his great big teeth.

'You know what what?' I asked him, mad at him for being so silly and babyish and toothy, even though I knew exactly what it was that was making him like that. And he stuck out his stomach as full as it would go without him actually falling over, and kept looking up at me and giggling, his face all red and shiny. 'Stop being stupid,' I snapped at him. 'I haven't a clue what you're on about.'

'I bet Chris has,' he giggled.

Grandad had been swimming. He caught up with us just as we got to his gate, and he jumped over the wall so he could beat us up the path. He bowed us in and his dog catapulted into us and tried to bowl us over.

'Watch it,' Grandad said, and he put out his hand to steady me. He slid it down my shoulder to my waist, the way he does, and I could feel him tensing. I wear loose clothes, they hide a lot. Now he would surely know.

'Grandad . . .' I began, but he lifted his hand away and without looking at me followed Robbie into the kitchen. I couldn't make myself follow him. I went straight upstairs to see my nan. She likes to sit by her window staring out at the street through a crack in the curtains. I can't imagine what it is that she thinks about all the time. It's as if she slipped into old age without even realizing. She's hard work. I sit and talk to her even though I feel uncomfortable with her. I feel sorry for her. Her eyes are always sad. What frightens me most is that Mum is a bit like that sometimes, a tiny bit, especially these days, as if deep inside her head her own thoughts are much more interesting than what's going on around her.

Grandad and Robbie came in with the sandwiches and put them on the little table that Nan uses. Grandad kissed her on her permed hair as he put the tray down, then went downstairs again, whistling something without a tune between his teeth. He came back up with a glass vase and some roses from his garden. 'Here, Dorrie, smell,' he told her, and she shifted her sad eyes round to him for a minute and shook her head and then looked away again.

'What d'you think of England's chances, then?' Grandad asked Robbie, and they settled down to talk about the

World Cup, and I sauntered over to the window with a wedge of cheese sandwich in my hand and stood looking out at the kids playing in the street. You could just hear their voices, echoing against the bricks. It would rain again soon. The air had that kind of hollowness about it.

And then Nan said, 'When's that baby of yours due?'

Grandad and Robbie stopped talking immediately. I could feel Grandad's eyes on me. I made myself look up at him.

'What are you on about, Dorrie?' Grandad said. 'This is little Helen you're talking to.'

Nan just kept her eyes fixed on me, chewing on a sandwich crust.

'I'm not little Helen.' I could hardly talk, I'd started shaking so much. 'Nan's right, Grandad.'

Robbie started giggling again.

'I don't know,' Nan sighed. 'There must be bad blood in our family. Like mother, like daughter.'

★ ★ ★

On the afternoon of our last exam Tom and I went out on our bikes. I've never cycled so far and so fast all in one go, ever. We scorched through the Hope Valley to Castleton, and slogged our way up Winnats Pass. My heart felt like a red, swelling balloon, blown up to burst. Brilliant, Winnats Pass. You feel as if you'll never climb out of it, and suddenly you're up and into air and light and you're coasting free as water all the way to Buxton. We were yelling our heads off going downhill.

'Let's hit Wildboarclough!' Tom shouted, and we bombed off head-down out to the moors, never seeing a car or a bike or a hiker. Plenty of sheep up there. Plenty of curlews, rippling away like rivers. We flung ourselves off our bikes when we got to the top and emptied our water bottles down our throats.

'Hell,' said Tom, flat on his back with his shirt off and his tracksuit trows rolled up to his knees. 'You've got to come to France next month, Dope-head.'

'Can't.'

'Why the hell not? I'll lend you the dosh if you're short.'

'It's not that.'

'What then? Helen? She'll not stop you.'

I wanted to tell him then about Helen. I didn't know how to say it. I've got Helen pregnant. Helen's having a kid. We're having a baby. I hadn't got the vocabulary for it, and that was the truth. I'd spent the last two weeks scribbling thousands of useless words on to exam papers and I couldn't bring out the most significant sentence in my life.

'She's okay is Helen,' Tom said. 'What d'you reckon? Will you two stay the course?'

I pretended to laugh. 'Newcastle's a long way from Sheffield,' I said. And then I said, 'We might have to, though,' really quiet, changing my voice because it was thickened in my throat like treacle. That should have been enough for anyone; but not for old Tom-boy. He didn't say a word. How can someone who's been predicted to get three As be so dense?

Tom cycled on ahead and I slowed down to look over the valley. I knew that before the month was up Helen and I must have our talk, must decide what we should do. I felt a tingling of nerves as I started coasting down Wildboarclough, picking up speed as I went, just holding myself back with the lightest touch on the brakes, just leaning into the bends. There it was, spread before me, the huge vast green landscape, and no way of seeing over the edge, or beyond the blue hills. If I eased off the brakes I'd hurtle down into space, into nothing, into amazing calm.

A couple of days later we had the sixth-form farewell do. Actually it was an alternative do arranged by Tom, because half of them wanted to go to a disco in town which is usually full of forty-year-old blokes trying to get off with sixteen-year-old girls. It's pathetic. It makes me ill. So Tom suggested that we burn off to hear a Zambian band playing at the Leadmill. About ten of us went, including Helen and Ruthlyn. We would have to make some plan soon, I knew that. I had no idea what we would decide to do.

Helen was in a weird state, right from the moment we set off. She was as brittle as glass. I couldn't fathom her mood that night. One minute she was holding my hand and letting me kiss her and the next minute she was cold and quiet, a million miles away. She tortures me when she's like this. I didn't know what the hell was going on. I didn't know till the end of the evening, till I was walking her home.

She looked fantastic. She was wearing something loose and blue and floating, and her hair was soft and gleaming, always catching the light, wherever she moved. When the band started playing they all got up to dance but I just watched Helen. You should see her dancing. Everyone watches her. She pretends she doesn't know, and she dances with her eyes half closed, and every so often she'd glance at me and give me that amazing smile of hers. There was no one else in the room as far as I was concerned.

While I was watching her I had an idea. It was such a perfect idea, and it just floated into the air, so thrilling and obvious that I wanted to shout it out to her over the music. I held it in my head, though. I went over to her and started dancing, full of it. I decided to tell her on the way home. It was this: I would ask to have my university place transferred to Sheffield. It was so simple.

★ ★ ★

June 23rd

Dear Nobody,

I knew it had to be tonight.

I tried to make it the best night we'd ever had together. I tried to let Chris know that he was the most special person in the world. Every now and again I remembered what it was I was going to have to say to him at the end of the evening. It kept rising up in me, as if it was going to drown me. I kept smiling at him to tell him everything was all right. He was watching me all the time. I knew he was anxious. He knew something was up.

The Zambian band was playing such buoyant, happy music. They were all laughing and cheerful. You can't resist dancing to music like that. The rhythm seems to go right into your blood and bones. Everyone was dancing – old men and kids. Our group loved it. I was wearing a very loose dress and I was dancing just for Chris. I knew people were watching me, and I knew for sure that it was obvious now that I was pregnant. I knew the exact moment when Tom realized. He went absolutely white. He looked at Chris, and then at me, and I smiled at him. 'It's all right, Tom,' I wanted to tell him. 'It's all right.'

Chris sat for ages just watching me. I think he was miles away. I don't think he even saw the ripples of knowing that were passing through Tom and the others. He suddenly jumped up and came over to me and let himself go. His feet go wild when he dances. You'd think he'd tied them on to the ends of his fingers with elastic bands. He has no co-ordination at all. How he stays on his bike I don't know. And all the time he was dancing and throwing his feet round I was thinking how much I like him, little Nobody. I can't say that other word. It's too dangerous. It hurts and hurts and hurts.

It was nearly as light as day when we came out. We were all together at first and then everyone seemed to melt away in twos and groups and it was just me and Chris, arms round each other, walking as slow as smoke to make the miles stretch out. I wanted it to last forever. I didn't want to say what I knew I would have to say.

And Chris said to me, at the corner of our road, 'Nell, we shouldn't have to say goodnight to each other. We should be together all the time now.'

And that was when I told him.

Helen

You have no right to do this to me. You can't shut me out of your life, now. You can't keep me away. I won't stay away.

I threw that one in the bin.

Darling Nell

I love you.

And that.

Helen

You can't mean it. Please don't mean it. Please see me again. Please let's talk.

And that.

I wrote them all again, and posted them in one envelope. I wrote every day. She didn't answer. She hadn't got the decency to answer. Suddenly I didn't exist. Suddenly fifty per cent of that baby was deleted for ever. She didn't even ask me what I wanted. She just told me what she wanted and walked away, out of my life, into a room with a locked door. Ruthlyn told me Helen was upset. Too damned right she should be upset. She'd locked me out from the start. That was what I realized then. She'd made every decision on her own, as if it had nothing to do with me.

And when I wasn't feeling anger, I was feeling despair. I was helpless to do anything. I was adrift in space, and looking at Earth, looking at Helen; I was a million miles away and I was in exile.

My dad heard me crying one night. He didn't give me the old clichés about plenty more fish in the sea, or I'd get over it, and I was better off without her, or even big boys don't cry. Nothing like that. He came in and sat on the chair by my bed and touched my shoulder, just to let me know he was there, and he said I might fancy watching Ireland playing Romania later, and he'd save a pint for me. I just watched the play-off penalties. For five whole minutes I forgot about Helen. Almost.

Tom asked me to come and watch England and Belgium in the semi-final on the big screen at the Poly. We went to the climbing wall first. I just sat and watched him. All those voices round me, echoing like sleep. All those students moving about and laughing and acting as if nothing had happened. I couldn't believe they didn't know, that they didn't care. I felt as if I was drowning in some grey, gluey paste. I followed Tom out like an old man.

'You're as miserable as sin,' Tom said.

'Get lost, Tom,' I said.

'She's a cow to do this to you,' he said.

I nearly hit him. If he hadn't been bigger than me, and strong enough to hold my arm back, I'd have punched his nose in. He put his arm across my shoulder and steered me into the Mandela Building. It was crowded with students, about a thousand of them at least, all sitting round watching the match on a big screen. I sat like a gawping fish all through the game, Helen's face floating in front of the screen, Helen laughing, Helen tilting back her head, Helen dancing with her eyes closed and her hair drifting across her face. Suddenly, in the last minute of extra time, England scored. It was like a shot from a gun – bang! straight into goal. Clean as ice. I was up on my feet and yelling with the rest of them. I didn't even know I was doing it. The whole room was up, screaming their heads off, waving their arms about. We never heard the commentary after that. We barged out of the Mandela Building with our arms in the air yelling and cheering our heads off, about a thousand of us storming down the Moor, waving our arms in the air. It was like being swept along in a tide. We were delirious. England, England! I was shouting.

I don't remember getting home that night.

I was sick. I remember that.

July

When I knew that she really meant it the only thing I could think about was getting away. After I'd spent days cycling up and down her road, waiting round our old haunts in town and going to our special places to look out for her, the places all turned sour on me. I couldn't bear the thought of being there without her. The Leadmill, the record shops, Fox House, the bar at Atkinson's where we used to drink hot chocolate; I hated them all. I dreaded the thought of bumping into her and her not talking to me. I was afraid I might break down or do something stupid if I saw her. Everywhere I went was haunted by Helen. Every time I got on a bus I expected her to be on it. Every time I went into a room I thought she'd be in it. She inhabited all the spaces of Sheffield, yet she wasn't there. She was nowhere. She'd been spirited away from my life, and the best part of me had gone with her.

So when Tom came round one day and sat with me in

the yard for a bit and said, 'The offer's still on, Chris. If you'd like to come to France, I'll lend you the dosh,' I rose up out of my coma and said, 'Yes, I'll go.'

I wish I hadn't.

* * *

Dear Nobody,

Today I was sitting on my bed with all these letters to you spread round me, and Chris's photograph in my hand, and Mum came into the room. She stood in the doorway with some clean sheets for my bed folded over her arms and watched me. I could feel her eyes on me. I kept thinking about what my nan had said, 'Like mother, like daughter.' What did she mean, Mum? I wanted to say, and daren't. And I wanted to say, I've finished with Chris. Help me, Mum.

I was looking at Chris's photograph for the last time because I had decided to put it away, out of sight, out of mind. She just stood there saying nothing and then she came over to my bed. I couldn't look at her. I wanted to reach out to her and tell her. If she stops in my room, I thought, I'll tell her. For a moment she hesitated by my bed, and I knew she was looking at the photograph and wondering, perhaps, at all these letters. For a moment it seemed as if she was going to say something. We were in a web of silence in that room, and something was swaying between us, spinning strands from one to the other. I was afraid to move or to breathe in case the strands broke. She leaned forward, very slightly, and put my clean sheets on my bed, covering the letters, covering his photograph, and as I looked up she walked out of the room, head bowed a little, and closed the door behind her.

* * *

Tom and I left for France very early on the 11th of July, exactly twenty days after Helen finished with me. It was a terrible journey. I got a puncture cycling to the station, the guard didn't want us to put our bikes in the goods van even though we'd paid for them, the train broke down so by the time we reached London it was the rush hour and we had to cycle through death traffic to get to Victoria Station, and Tom was sick on the ferry. But at last we were in France. We were training it down to the Loire Valley, then doing a sort of cross-France tour, finishing up in the Alps and cycling home at the end of the month. Hippy Harrington had given us some books at the end of the exams – his bibles, he called them. One of them was called *Zen and the Art of Motorcycle Maintenance.* 'Is it a manual?'

Tom asked me. 'Not much point having a manual for motorbikes.' 'Is it hell,' I said. 'It's a pillow and it's about the pain of existence.' I think it kept me sane, that book. Tom was hopeless. He'd happily do all the shopping and cooking and put both tents up rather than get his spanners out and mend his bike, so I did all that. Helps you to think, anyway, about life, I suppose. Brings you down to basics, when you have to cope with staying alive. Sometimes I found that I was really happy. I wouldn't have believed it possible. We'd be cycling down one of those amazing straight French roads with fields and fields of massive yellow sunflowers on either side of us and only birds to hear, or Tom chanting away on his bike, and the long, hot day stretching in front of us and behind us, and I'd realize that I felt completely happy. When I finished reading Zen at night and put my torch out and lay listening to owls in the dark: that was when the aching started up.

'Chris,' Tom said to me one night. His tent was pitched a couple of metres away. 'Are you awake?'

'No.'

'Are you still missing her?'

'Christ, Tom!'

'You're not snoring so I knew you were awake.'

He put his torch on and crawled over to my tent on his belly, still in his sleeping bag. He unzipped my tent and we both sat in the opening. The stars were huge. We could hear a stream trickling near by. The night seemed to be full of noises, bumping into each other, starting up out of the darkness.

'Hear that dog?' Tom asked.

'Fox, I bet,' I said.

'Bet you're right.'

There was a hare or something too, trapped out there, crying like a child.

'Finished your book?' he asked.

'Nah. Savouring it. It's good.'

'I'm reading that Kerouac book. *On the Road*.'

'Another of Hippy's recommendations.'

'Can't believe it was written in 1959, though! I mean, it's a history book!'

'But maybe all kids want to get out in wagons and burn off across the horizon,' I said. 'Maybe that's why it still works.'

'It sold eighteen million copies, that book. That says something, I suppose. That means eighteen million kids have read it and wanted to drive vast distances and turn their heads over and meet themselves again at the other side.' We were lying on our backs now with our sleeping bags tucked up round us and our hands under our heads, looking up at the sky, like a pair of caterpillars that had been rolled over the wrong way. 'Are they chasing something or running away from something?'

I rolled over. Those stars were too bright to look at, too hard and cold and icy. 'I reckon they're just going somewhere, anywhere, just for the hell of it.'

'Is there anywhere to go, anyway?'

Tom and I talked for hours about it. Anyway, ten years after he wrote it, Jack Kerouac was dead. Drank himself into oblivion. That says something too, I suppose. That's another kind of journey. All the time we were talking, drifting to sleep and waking up and talking again, Helen was there, right in front of my mind, brighter than the stars.

★ ★ ★

July 17th

Dear Nobody,

I can't believe it's the middle of July, and that you have been inside me now for six months. It's no secret now, however loose my dresses are. It would be like trying to stop day coming, if I tried to hide you now. You keep pushing out with your leg or your arm, as if you're trying to wave in there, to say hey! I'm here! You're not taking any notice of me. But I'm thinking about you all the time. I can't take my mind off you.

And it's so hot! We're in the middle of a heatwave. I feel as if I'm trudging along with a bag of shopping tied round my middle. I try to imagine you, in the cool sea cave that's your home. Is it like being in a dark rock pool, turning over and over with the tide of my beating heart? Are you calm in there, and all crouched up safe? You're a real person. I can't wait to see you.

Oh, but these are happy daytime thoughts, little Nobody. Night after night now I wake up lonely and afraid. I went out into the garden last night. The sky was clear, the stars looked enormous. I could hear the hum of the city, even at that time, the drone of traffic. Everywhere, everywhere in the world, people were on the move, people were dying, people were being born. Our garden was full of shadows, trees and moonlight and shadows, silver and velvet, lonely, quiet, humming shadows. I wanted to scream out into them. What will I do? I don't know where we're going to live, or what we're going to live on. I don't know how to look after you. I don't know if I'm strong enough for this. I'm frightened of the dark. And when I turned back into the house, into the kitchen with all its gleaming, useful machinery, all its domestic reassurances, I was frightened of the light. I don't know anything. I want Chris to hold me in his arms and say, it's all right, we'll manage, we can do it together. But I've turned my back on all that, and nothing will stop day coming, nothing will stop you being born. You'll march into the world bursting with power and wisdom because you know how to be born. I don't know anything.

I closed the curtains because I couldn't bear to look at the sky; it was growing light: dawn was coming, and nothing, nothing would stop it.

★ ★ ★

The next day Tom pigged at me for snoring all night and keeping him awake. We were both so tired that it took us two hours to have breakfast and pack the tents and load the bikes.

'We can't mess around like this all the time,' I grumbled. I wanted to get my head down and ride like the wind, kind of punishing myself. Tom was just there for a laze. We sneaked into a campsite and had a shower, which felt brilliant, and the next night a farmer, who told us his name was Monsieur Bienvenu, let us come on his field for free. We talked to him for ages, watching him while he milked his cows. I'm not kidding, that milk came out hot and steaming! I've never seen or smelt anything like it. He dipped a jug into the churn and ladled some out for us to drink. It tasted like grass. Tom's French is desperate but when he doesn't know a word he just makes one up and says it in a French accent and he gets away with it. I take hours trying to sort out the tense and working out whether the nouns are masculine or feminine and by the time I've got the sentence right it's too late to say it because they're on about something else, so even though I'm the one doing French A level he did most of the talking and I just prodded words into spaces. The farmer's wife gave us some home-made orange liqueur and after that the talking was easier and the jokes started flying. I think we drank it too fast.

The next day we were cycling through some town or other with headaches and had to remind ourselves that the traffic all goes in a different direction and that roundabouts are death traps. I kept imagining Helen hearing that I'd been killed in France. Would you feel sorry then, disdainful Nell? At night it was too hot to sleep. I was sunburnt and saddle sore. I'd got baguette blisters inside my mouth. Every girl I saw looked like Helen.

I bought three postcards. One for Dad. One for my mother. And one for Jill.

★ ★ ★

Dear Nobody,
    'Nan,' I said, 'tell me about when you were a little girl.'

Her room was nearly in darkness, even though it was glorious day outside. She had her curtains pulled to keep out the sunlight. I hated its stuffiness; always have done.

'When I was a little girl? What d'you want to know about that for?'

I wanted to know everything, Nobody. I want to peer into all the corners.

'Did you live in Sheffield?'

She tittered unexpectedly. 'I lived in a drawer.'

I knew this already. Long ago, when I was a little girl, she'd told me that, but she'd never gone on to tell me what she meant. I waited in the silence. Outside in the garden Grandad was cutting the hedge, whistling.

'In them days, if you couldn't afford cradle nor cot, you put your bairns in a drawer. Good enough, I'd say.'

Well, I was thinking, I'll do the same if I have to, only I'll be sure to line it with soft things first, and she said, 'And anyway, what better place to hide me, eh? If I cried too much, or if the lady from upstairs wanted to visit the kitchens, my mother just had to push the drawer, and I'd disappear. Very handy, if you think about it.' She laughed again, her little, light, tittering laugh that seems to come from a little girl rather than a woman in her seventies.

'But she didn't do it, Nan, did she?'

She glanced over to me sharply. 'It wasn't that she wasn't married, if that's what you're thinking. She was married to the butler. But she wasn't allowed to have a child, you see, not while she was in service. She'd have lost her job. So I was a secret.'

'But she didn't close the drawer?'

Nan closed her eyes. She clasped her hands together tight under her chest, and tucked her chin down. Her voice came out in little whispers. 'I believe I can remember it now. Shelves right up there, stacked with black pots. I can hear the sounds of skirts and footsteps and voices. I can remember daylight changing into dark across my face, like that.' She moved her hands in front of her eyes, so her eyelids trembled slightly, then she clasped them together again across her chest. 'I can remember sliding, and a sudden jolting. Crack! And I can smell it, too, stuffy and sweet.'

'Weren't you frightened?'

'Too young to be frightened,' she said, in a little whimpering voice. 'Besides, I like the dark.'

I went out to see Grandad. I wanted to help him to sweep up the hedge clippings but he wouldn't let me, so I sat on a stool in the sunshine and watched him. He grunted every time he stooped.

'Nan's asleep,' I told him.

'Ay ay,' he said. 'She'll sleep till teatime now.'

'Can't you get her to sit out here sometimes?'

'She will, when she feels like it. She'll be as chirpy as a sparrow tomorrow, maybe. But when she's a mood on, nowt'll shift her.'

'My mum never comes here, does she?' I said.

Grandad grunted. His cheeks purpled slightly when he bent down. I wish he'd let me help him. The privet smelt sharp and sweet as he brushed it.

'She's a mind of her own. She comes when she fancies to.'

'Were you pleased when she married my dad?'

You see what it was like, Nobody. I wanted to know everything. I've never dared ask questions like this before. Grandad leaned on his garden brush, blowing his lips out a little. He wiped the sweat off his forehead with the back of his hand. 'We thought it was a strange match, him being so reserved, you know. She had a bit of spirit about her. We thought, this'll never suit our Alice. Your mother was always one for schooling and bettering herself, all that palaver. I think she thought your dad was rather posh, being a university librarian. But I think he's been a bit of a disappointment to her.'

'Why's that?' I felt disloyal, talking about them like this, as if they were strangers, yet I was itchy to know about them. 'I think Dad's crazy about Mum.'

'Oh, ay. He'd do anything for her. Anything for a quiet life, I reckon,' Grandad chuckled. 'But he let her down over the dancing.'

'Dancing?'

He was sweeping vigorously now, chasing bits of twigs down the path. I slipped off my stool and followed him.

'Mad on dancing, your mother. Didn't you know that? When she was a kid she used to frisk round the house like a fairy.' He laughed again, shaking his head at the memory of it. 'Twirling all sorts round with her – ribbons, scarves, string, anything. She used to cut strips of toilet roll or newspaper and use them as streamers! Anything. She met your dad at a jazz club. He was the pianist, just a night job, you know. She used to go down there a lot, with her friends. Dancing. She was a classy dancer, your mother. I reckon that's what made him fall for her.'

I tried to imagine it: dim lights and smoke, Dad sitting in his shirtsleeves at the piano playing ragtime; Mum . . . ? No, I couldn't picture Mum.

'But why did he let her down?'

'I'm not so sure . . . he seemed to put his foot down, once they were married. Stopped her going to the club, anyway. That's the only time I've seen him do anything like that. Shy man, you see, your dad. Didn't like that sort of exhibitionism, probably. Not in a wife.'

'I never knew about that,' I said.

'Ay, well.' He was intent on watching a pair of sparrows taking a dust bath in the middle of his sweepings, squabbling together. 'There's lots of things about parents that kids never imagine, I reckon.' He thrust the brush forward and the sparrows lifted themselves up, still squabbling, and flew off in opposite directions. Grandad swept up the last of the leaves and dusted his hands on his trouser legs. 'People will get wed. They think it's going to open up the world for them. But it doesn't, you see. It closes all the doors.'

He heaved the garden sack round to the back to tip on the bonfire pile. 'Won't burn yet,' he grunted. 'Too green. Besides, I like to light bonnies in the evening, just on dusk. Nice and quiet, sitting out here on my own, watching the woodsmoke curl. Can't beat the smell of woodsmoke, Helen. And d'you know, when I'm sitting out here, just me and the midges and the bonfire crackling, there's a toad that comes and squats by me, just there, where you're standing, that far from the flames! Sits there blinking and swallowing, just watching it, little bright eyes yellow with flames. Thinking daft thoughts, same as me, I reckon. You'd think it would be too hot for him, wouldn't you!' He shook his head. 'Funny old thing, that is.'

'I'd better be getting back, Grandad,' I said. I didn't want to go, really. I love being with him.

'Helen . . .' as he bent down to kiss me, ' . . . is he going to marry you, that lad?'

I looked away. 'No, Grandad. I don't want to get married.'

'He's a nice lad, but he's young. You're too young for this, both of you.'

'I know. It's done now.'

He walked back up the path with me, stooping to pick up the bits of privet that had dropped out of the sack, splaying them out in his hand like a bridal spray. 'I know your mother. She won't be making it easy for you. If you want a home, Helen, you and your bairn . . . it's not much of a place, is this. I'd love it.'

I nodded.

'You could come here. Remember that.'

We've had a long journey today, little Nobody. We seem to have walked for miles and miles and miles, in all kinds of strange spaces. I feel a few steps nearer to Mum, anyway. But there's a long way to go yet, and lots more questions to ask.

Looking back on that holiday in France, I can only explain what happened by blaming it on circumstances. I'm not making excuses for myself.

On that day, the day that it started, we'd been going about two weeks and my bike was giving me major problems. The back wheel was buckled and the tyre kept rubbing on the frame. The gears were slipping, we were doing murderous hill climbs, I had sunburn and bum-ache. We searched round for a bike shop and when we found it it was closed because it was Monday. We sat on the pavement eating baguettes. My mouth was so cut up with the crusts by then that I could only eat the middle bits. There was no way I could fix the bike properly. All the spokes were loose. Some of them had gone through the rim and punctured the tyre. I reckon someone must have walked over the back wheel at the last campsite. Persig calls these kind of things 'gumption traps' in *Zen*. I could think of more colourful epithets. Tom was useless. He was all for hitching a lift on a lorry and going back home. At last we made it to a pebbly campsite and spent two hours pitching my tent. Then I had a proper go at my back wheel. There was a spoke wound round the hub, and three others were hanging loose. Ten others looked as if they were ready to fall off any minute. We were grounded for a couple of days till I could fix the thing. I felt quite calm about it all, strangely enough.

Tom started to pitch his tent and we found a massive hole in his tent bag and half a dozen little ones in the outer tent. We couldn't believe it. I'd been carrying it in my pannier bag and one of the loose spokes must have gone through it. We cursed a bloody hell of a lot then. Tom was in a massive peeve, with the heat, with France, and most of all with me. But that wasn't the end of that day's events. He went to have a shower to calm down, and I emptied out my other pannier. My sleeping bag was covered in oil.

So. That night it started to rain. Tom was going to have to share my tent, and I was going to have to sleep without a bag. My back wheel was in bits where my feet would have to be. Two girls started to pitch their tent near us and because they were having trouble with all the pebbles too, and because he fancies himself and because we weren't talking much, anyway, Tom went over to help them. I sat and sulked and tried to read *The Restaurant at the End of the Universe*, which didn't make me laugh. The worst disco in the world started up on an island on the river next to the campsite. That DJ should have been flung in a bed of nettles. Tom went to it with the two girls. I pretended not to see them walk past, laughing their heads off at the terrible music. I couldn't read. After a bit I went down and watched. It was lousy. One of the girls saw me and waved to me to join them. I didn't. I went back to the tent, feeling terrible. She had a smile like Helen's.

Tom finally crawled into my tent long after midnight, and woke me up to tell me that I was winning 2–1 – his tent was as holy as a church, my back wheel was dropping to bits and I had a sleeping bag covered in chain-oil. He was remarkably cheerful about it all. 'And,' he said, as I drifted back towards sleep, 'I've fallen in love, Chris.'

The next day I spent ninety francs at a bike shop. I left the bike there first thing and spent the rest of the day reading. I finished *Restaurant* and started *Catcher in the Rye*. 'This will change your life,' Hippy had told me. Well, it needed changing. Tom and the two girls were messing about, playing with a frisbee and rounding up all the campsite dogs. They seemed to spend all their time laughing, annoying the hell out of me. The girls were Welsh. Bryn and Menai, they were called. They were hitching round France, which I think is a stupid thing for girls to do. They talked to each other in Welsh all the time, and that irritated me from the start. The little one, Bryn, was dark, and just wouldn't stop talking. I tried to ignore her but she seemed to know a lot about books and kept asking me which bit I was up to. I hate people talking to me when I'm reading. But every time I looked up, she had that incredible smile.

At six o'clock I went back into town to collect my bike. It was brilliant. I picked up some wine on the way back and we invited the girls over to eat with us. And in the evening that crazy disco started up again on the island and we went over to it.

It was fantastic!

* * *

July 23rd

Dear Nobody,

It's a month exactly since I finished with Chris. It isn't any easier. I can't stop thinking about him. I'm surprised I never bump into him; he doesn't live that far away from me. He seems to have disappeared off the face of the earth. Sometimes, Nobody, I used to feel years older than him. Sometimes I used to feel really impatient with him for being so romantic, so impractical. I know now that that's what I miss most about him. He would think that if he just put his arms round me and loved me, everything would be all right again. Sometimes, now, I almost believe that's true.

I talked to Mum this evening, at last. It wasn't easy. Dad was out with his band and Robbie was digging a hole in the back garden because he's decided we should do something for the environment and he's going to make a pond. The room was yellow with sun, I remember that. I asked Mum if she'd like a glass of sherry, which amazed her, but she giggled and said yes. I had orange juice, of course, piled with ice cubes. No alcohol for you, little tadpole!

I told Mum that I'd finished with Chris for good. I let the hurt come out then, in front of Mum, when I was telling her. She listened quietly. She didn't hug me, or anything, of course. She doesn't know how to. I was glad she didn't. I wanted to be in control of this.

I told her that I didn't want to get married or live with him and I didn't think Chris and I should tie each other down. Most of all, I told her, I did it because I thought that Chris would be crazy to give up his university place. I didn't want to be responsible for that, I told her. The easiest way to do it was to make the break now. I know that speech off by heart.

Mum sat very quiet for a long time, sipping at her sherry as if she was kissing the glass almost, just damping her lips with it. She asked me again to think about having you adopted and I said, very firmly, as I say every time, no. You kicked a bit then. I'm sure you can hear what I'm saying. And she just nodded and sighed a little but there was none of that other stuff, that emotion and stuff.

'Then what are you going to do?' she asked me, and I told her that I would try for a university or college place in Sheffield to do a music degree when you're old enough to go to the crèche there. Maybe they would even let me reapply to Manchester to do Composition one day. She pulled a face as if she thought I was mad to think such things are possible. But they are possible. I just know they are. A baby isn't the end of everything. It's the beginning of something else. Then I said that I knew she wouldn't want me to live at home once you were born, and that Grandad had said I could have a room at his house if I wanted it. Her eyebrows shot up then. She hardly ever goes there. I don't think she likes her mother. Or maybe she doesn't like her the way she is now, an old woman before her time, daydreaming the years away. Well, that's what I thought. I found out that it was something much deeper than that, something much more powerful, that kept her away.

'That's no place for a baby,' she said.

And then I told her what Nan had said.

I'd spent days rummaging through all the papers in Mum and Dad's box files, trying to find my birth certificate and their wedding certificate. I don't know where they'd hidden them. I felt like a thief in the night, touching forbidden things. And after a bit, when my search was fruitless and yet I searched again and again in the same places, I began to feel quite feverish about it, as if part of my life was lost and would never be found again. And because she sat there, so still and shocked, sipping at an empty sherry glass, I asked, brave as anything, Nobody, if I was born before she was married. She closed her eyes and shuddered, as if she was suddenly cold to the bone. We could hear Robbie outside, singing as he was digging. He would be so hot, out there. Any minute now he'd come in for water and would flop on to the settee, legs sprawled out in front of him, staring from one to the other of us, knowing he was missing something. Somewhere in the room a bluebottle was buzzing. I think it was trapped in the curtains.

Mum said no, of course not, they'd been married for two years before I was born. She picked up a letter that was lying on the table in front of her and started fanning herself with it. 'This dreadful heat,' she said.

I was a dog on the scent now, digging away, sending all the muck flying up. 'But there was a baby, wasn't there? Nan said, "Like mother, like daughter." What did she mean?'

I had to find out, Nobody, for you. It seemed to be part of your past, and part of our future.

'If it wasn't me, who was it? Where is it now?'

She said it was none of my business, and calm as anything, feeling that deep inside I was the same person as she was, just as you're the same person as I am, just as she is the same person as that quiet, sad old woman staring all day and all life out of a crack in her bedroom curtains, I told her that I thought it *was* my business.

'What are you trying to ask me, Helen?' she said at last, and I told that from what my nan had said it sounded as if I'd been born illegitimate. I was sure that was what she had meant. I told her the words: 'bad blood'. It was a hard thing to say. 'Like mother, like daughter.' I was hurting myself, too. I was hurting you.

'Do you imagine I'd do a thing like that?' she said then, her voice gone cold and shaking. 'A dirty thing like that?'

No. After all I couldn't imagine it. Not if she thought it was dirty. How can love be dirty? If she'd said sinful, or silly, or thoughtless, it wouldn't have hurt so much as that word 'dirty' did. For a minute I was sidetracked. I asked her if she'd ever been in love, then, which I suppose was a bit of an impertinence. But she's so difficult to talk to. She's such a closed-up, tight woman at times. I can't imagine her being the same age as me, ever. She won't give anything, just as she won't take anything from me.

'Well. Were you in love with Dad when you married him?' Why couldn't she answer that, at least, instead of sitting there with her mouth all pursed up, fanning herself with her eyes closed, locked away from me? I wanted to see Alice, the girl that she was, the me in her at eighteen or so. And she couldn't answer that question, or wouldn't. Does that mean she did or she didn't? I remembered Mum then as she used to be when I was a kid, at Christmastime perhaps when she'd had a drink or two. I remembered watching her once, shimmying round the kitchen in an odd, flappy dance that had made Robbie and me laugh. My dad was watching her, too, in a half-proud, half-disapproving way, and she had danced up to him and put both her hands on his shoulders and danced just for him, holding his eyes in hers, and both of them gone quiet as night, till I'd felt embarrassed and locked out. Things like that didn't happen any more.

And then, just when I'd given up and I was about to go out of the room, she said, 'If you must know, Helen, I'm the one who was illegitimate, not you.'

The bluebottle had gone still. Even Robbie had stopped his maniac singing. 'I was born out of wedlock, as they say. Born in sin. And I'll never forgive my mother for that.'

That was when the talking started, little Nobody.

'I don't even know who my father is,' she said. 'Except, Helen, that he was a dancer in a nightclub. It was your father who found that out.'

I was utterly shocked at this news. I walked over to the window and watched Robbie at his digging. One of his friends had come round to help him. They'd stripped off their tee shirts. I could see how their shoulders were looking pink and sore already.

'So Grandad isn't really . . .' I couldn't take it in. I felt closer to my grandfather than to any other member of my family; always had done.

'He married her when I was about nine. And that, I can tell you, was a brave and generous thing to do. In those days an unmarried mother was no more than a slut. Her child was a disgrace. My mother's family wouldn't own her. She was an outcast, and so was I. A bastard, that's what you were called if you didn't have a father. That's what I was called, when I was a child at school. That's the start I had in life.'

It was as if she'd taken all the guilt of it on herself, all the family shame, and tried to put things right all through her life. I understood her then, for the first time in my life. I understood her commitment to that word 'decency' which was a word she cradled as if it was a gem, a precious legacy from another age. I was more shocked and confused by all this than if she'd told me what I thought had been the case, that I was born before she was married, or that she'd had a baby before she had me, or anything like that. Because what she was telling me was something that she had had no choice about, and that she wished had never happened. We have no choice about being born, little Nobody. I've made up your mind for you.

It's not a stigma any more, not like it was when Mum was a child. No one will be calling you names.

But I hope you'll forgive me, all the same.

★ ★ ★

Bryn gave me a Barry Hines book that she'd just finished reading. I said I knew him because he lives in Sheffield. I don't really, but I've seen his photograph in *The Star*. It was a goodbye present, she said, because we were heading off for Burgundy that day. 'Maybe we'll see you there,' she said. 'I hope we do.'

I didn't say anything.

So we left the Dordogne for the day to whip down to the Auvergne and spent it looking at mountains and taking photographs while Tom talked on and on about Menai. That night we camped on the top of a windy hill. It was bitterly cold, especially for me, minus my sleeping bag. We seemed to be a million miles away from civilization. The campsite woman had eyes like a cod and Tom christened her the Fish at the End of the Universe. 'I want Menai!' he kept saying. 'I can't live without her.'

'I thought you didn't believe in love,' I reminded him. 'You always told me changing girlfriends was as easy as changing your socks.'

'That was before love gave me blisters. I'm bleeding for her, Chris.'

'Get stuffed,' I said. 'Love's about as much use as a flat tyre on a mountain bike.'

I think, at the time, I meant it.

* * *

July 27th

Dear Nobody,

Today Mum and I went to town together. 'I want to buy you something nice, Helen,' she said, just as simply as that. It was really hot and you didn't help – you kept doing a limbo dance, waving your hands about or something. We went to Cole's first and looked at the materials there. 'D'you like this?' she asked me, stroking some blue, soft material.

'It's lovely, Mum,' I said. We have that in common. We both love fabrics and colours. When I was little she used to make all my clothes for me.

'Then I'll buy it,' she said. 'And we'll make a loose dress for you, to keep you cool.'

She could have bought me a maternity dress; any number. But it wouldn't have been the same, and I knew it.

We went to Atkinson's then, to the chocolate bar that Chris and I used to go to. I half expected to see him there. I half didn't want to go. In a way it was like exorcizing a ghost, walking into the place, sitting down, taking in his absence for a fact. We had toasted teacakes and hot chocolate with cream floating on the top.

'I used to come here with Chris,' I told her. I said it because at that moment I felt close to her. We used to have days like this together, years ago, when I was about eight. She would leave Robbie at home with Dad and she would take me to town to look at the shops and to buy materials for my dancing shows.

'I expect you did,' she said. 'There used to be a place like this near the old station that your father used to take me to, years ago.' She smiled. 'There used to be a jazz trio playing there. We spent hours there, holding hands, making one cup of chocolate last all afternoon.'

Chris and I used to listen to rock on my personal stereo in here, both sets of headphones plugged in. He used to forget himself sometimes and sing out loud to it. Or perhaps he did it on purpose, just to make me laugh.

On the way back to the bus stop I saw Jill. She didn't recognize me at first and I didn't really want to speak to her, in fact I felt deeply embarrassed, remembering what had happened last time I saw her. How could I have done that to you, little Nobody, that monstrous thing? I was another person then, slightly mad, I think, a frightened little girl, an animal in a trap. I was embarrassed about what she'd told Chris and me about herself, too, that precious, intimate secret. I wanted to tell her about my escape, our escape, from that clinic place. Well, I suppose she could tell, actually. She only had to look at me to know about you.

It feels as if a thousand years have passed since I last saw her. I didn't know how to introduce her to Mum, either, because she was so much part of my guilt and secrecy, and I was part of hers. I think she realized I was embarrassed so she chatted away about the horses at the stables and then, when our bus came and she was just about to walk away, she said, 'I had a postcard from France this morning. He's having a great time, isn't he?'

So that's where he is. Doesn't he care, then? Can he just go on holiday and forget about us?

My head was tumbling with all kinds of confused emotions. I didn't understand myself. I wanted to run away and hide, be on my own somewhere, open up my thoughts like a locked room and wander about in them. The day was spoilt, and all that lovely warmth that had been growing between Mum and me had gone. I was too wrapped up in myself to talk. I'd gone kind of tongue-tied, couldn't think of anything to say, couldn't bring myself to answer her questions about anything. I know she was disappointed. I was too. I didn't know what to do with myself. We sat in the garden for a bit and then she went in to cut out the dress for me. We should have done it together.

* * *

By the time we got to Burgundy Tom and I were beginning to feel we'd had enough. Some wino with a voice like a bassoon had fallen over my tent in the night and yanked all the guy ropes out, and rather than put it up in the dark I'd crawled in to Tom's. He was right about not changing his socks any more. They stank to high heaven. In the end I'd rolled them up in a ball and hurled them out of his tent. We found them in a pool of water the next morning.

'At least they've had a wash,' I told him.

We cruised at last into a little village that was

surrounded by fields full of white cows, and looked for the campsite.

'What wouldn't I give for a bed,' Tom moaned. 'Have you heard of those things, Chris?'

'What things?' I said. I'd seen something that he hadn't. A familiar tent. Two girls lying on their stomachs, reading.

'Wooden frames with mattresses and sheets and pillows. Widely used as an alternative to canvas stretched over mud and stones, apparently.'

He saw them too, then. He raised his fist to me and I raised mine. We couldn't stop grinning.

That night we sat in the dark, all four of us, drinking wine and looking up at the stars. We gave them names like Flash Harry and Sparky, Skylight and Brillo Pad and then we went through them in French and Bryn translated them into Welsh. She wants to be a writer. She's doing English next year, too, in Leeds. It's odd how much she reminded me of Helen, yet she was nothing like her at all.

We were supposed to be carrying on to the Alps the next day but we didn't. We didn't even talk about it. It's what old Tom called fate, I suppose. If only we'd gone to a different campsite.

Instead we went for a walk in absolutely sweltering midday heat, all along narrow winding cart tracks and past fields that were full of corn.

'It's made of gold, today,' Bryn said. She looked up at me and away again, biting her lip. 'I don't want it to end, ever.' She told me a poem in Welsh and started to explain about the complicated rhyming pattern of Welsh poetry. We were having a hell of a laugh trying to make up a poem in English that would work the same way and we suddenly realized that we'd lost Tom and Menai and that we hadn't a clue where we were. The heat was so intense that it was like walking through a furnace, and there were crickets all round us, chirring away incessantly. The air was heavy with the noise of them, a kind of intense clamouring. We walked down through some trees for shade and there was a river, like something from a dream. Bryn stripped off and jumped straight in. I couldn't believe it. Helen would never have done that, never in a million years, and there was Bryn just peeling off her clothes as if it was the most natural thing in the world to do and laughing back at me and splashing into the water. There wasn't a sound, except for insects humming and those crickets, chirring away.

'Come on, Chris,' Bryn called.

There were some cows paddling further down and some suspicious-looking brown stuff floating on the top so I didn't fancy it, but she kept trying to splash me so in the end I jumped in too. We swam up to the cows and they all turned their heads to look at us, all in a row, all big sad eyes. There were huge green and blue dragonflies zipping round us. Bryn said they were demoiselles. We climbed out and lay in the sun. I was almost afraid to look at her.

She told me that she and her boyfriend had packed up before she came away, and that she had never thought she'd be happy again, and that today had been fantastic. I told her about Helen.

'What's she like?' Bryn asked me.

Like a poem, I wanted to say, like a star, 'She's brilliant.'

'Oh,' Bryn laughed, 'too clever for you, then.'

I would have liked to tell her about the baby but I couldn't. I told her that Helen had said she didn't want to see me again, and she asked me if I was very hurt about it, and I said yes, very, and my voice cracked a bit then. We lay there without saying anything and the grass was full of poppies and butterflies and these huge green demoiselles and I was wondering what the hell I was going to do about the way I was beginning to feel and she just kind of rolled over in the grass towards me and put her arms out and began to kiss me.

Oh, Nell. I wanted you so much.

August

August 8th

Dear Nobody,

   It's too hot. I've turned into a tottering boat, a huge swaying galleon with round sails. Can I possibly get bigger than this and not burst? I saw a film once of a man stuffing himself with food till he exploded over all the people in the restaurant. I laughed at the time.

   And you don't help. You're nudging me and elbowing me all the time. I expect it's getting a bit cramped for you in there. Sometimes I think you're as big as a whale, lumbering up out of the sea, arching your great long back. I've heard a record of whales singing. They can hear each other forty miles apart in the ocean. I wonder if you're singing in there.

   I used to think oceans would be silent places. They must sound like motorways with all that whale-singing going on.

I'm being besieged by doctors and midwives and health visitors, monitoring my weight and your size and your heartbeat and my blood pressure, till I'm beginning to feel like a campaign rather than a person. They're taking me over. I'm scared that they're going to take you over, too. I dream that I'm lying in a bed in a hospital and that someone walks past me with a pram. I know that you're in it and that they're taking you away from me and I try to sit up but my arms and legs are weighted down, try to scream out but my mouth is bandaged up, and my mother sits at the side of the bed and smiles down at me.

I've been given breathing and relaxtion exercises to do but as soon as I start to do them I start shaking. Nobody, what's it going to be like, giving birth to you? However many people are with me on that day, I'll still be on my own with the pain. In my head I scream out loud, no one can hear me, they think I'm calm, that I'm not worrying. I sit in front of the television at home with Robbie and my face is quiet but in my head I'm screaming out loud.

Ruthlyn came to the relaxation class with me today. I hate going. I feel really out of it, without a partner, years younger than anyone. At least Ruthlyn sees the funny side of things. We giggled all the way to the clinic on the bus. People kept looking at us, as if we were invading their privacy just by laughing, then they sort of smiled at each other knowingly when they noticed me. You, I mean. I felt about twelve years old, Nobody. One woman actually patted my stomach as I got off the bus! What a cheek! How would she feel if I went and patted hers? 'You look bonny, love,' she said to me and patted my lump, you, as if she was a good witch charming me. I didn't feel bonny. My back aches and aches all the time, you're so heavy; my head is screaming inside.

At the antenatal clinic I had to lie on my back on the floor and breathe in and out, slowly and regularly, and curl round and move my legs up and down, very gently. I was really aware of you then. Some of the women had their husbands with them. There were all these bloated women on the floor having their ankles squeezed by partners and friends, trying to simulate labour pains. Ruthlyn did her best, trying to look solemn and practised, but every time she caught my eyes she cracked out laughing. It's all right for her. Laughing hurts. None of us took it seriously. It wasn't real. We were all as shy as each other and smiling at each other like kids at a new school. I felt embarrassed, yet I felt supported, too, by all of them. Embarrassed and embraced. That sounds nice, doesn't it? Afterwards we chatted about when our babies were due and suddenly, after all, it seemed terribly real. A few weeks away! It's really, really going to happen.

I can't wait to meet you.

I felt relaxed when I came out. I could have gone straight to sleep. You were dozing, for a change. Ruthlyn and I sat behind a young mother on the bus. Her baby kept peeping over the top of the seat at us, and we were both laughing at it and ducking our heads, trying to get it to smile at us. It looked so solemn, like a little old professor, just staring at us. I wonder what on earth it was thinking. Do babies have thoughts? Do you, in there? Or are thoughts only related to experience?

Then all of a sudden the baby had had enough of us, or of the journey, or of life, or something; anyway, it started howling. Its eyes puckered up and its cheeks bulged out like red balloons and its mouth turned into a black square and it screeched and yelled and howled, great ear-splitting volleys of sound like fireworks whooshing off. The poor mother tried everything – kissing it and shushing it and standing it up and rocking it and shoving the crook of her finger into its mouth, and in the end she was redder than the baby was and everyone on the bus was squirming about feeling hot and cross. I'm sure she got off before her stop. She just suddenly stood up, lugging her screaming bundle and her two bags of shopping with her. Her fold-up pram just wouldn't separate itself from all the other stuff in the luggage rack. I stood up to help her and she gave me a real sharing, hopeless, pitying sort of look. She didn't have a ring on either. Does that mean she lives on her own with her baby? And does it scream like that all night? I can still hear it now. Could you hear it, little Nobody? Did you respond to it, in your subsonic ocean voice?

Ruthlyn grinned at me when I sat down again. 'Little brat!' she whispered. 'Yours won't be like that, Helen.'

But Ruthlyn and I were miles apart by then. Miles and miles.

* * *

By the time the A level results came out France seemed a lifetime away. I cycled round to Tom's and we went down to school together. We could have had them sent through the post but quite honestly I don't think I'd have been able to open the envelope. We shook hands outside the door of the secretary's office just as we had done on the morning of the first exam. Mrs Price smiled at me and nodded towards the table where the results were spread out in little folded-up strips of paper. I couldn't find my name at first, then I couldn't find the marks on it, there was so much wording. I found English. A! I whooped out loud and Mrs Price chuckled. My heart started pumping again. I hadn't realized it had stopped. C for French. It stopped again. F for General. F! F! They must have made a mistake. My head was rapidly doing sums to count up the points and I realized there was one missing. I couldn't find it. I couldn't even remember what subject it was. I had to sit down for a bit. I needed three Bs for the course, and I hadn't got them. It was then that I knew for sure how much my English degree meant to me. I hadn't allowed myself to think about it up till now, not really. It hadn't been possible for me to focus properly on anything. Maybe being away had helped. Maybe Bryn had helped, in a strange, perverse, upside-down sort of way. And now it looked as if I'd lost my chance, after all. Old Fate again. It has a way of taking over your life, all right.

Mrs Price looked up from her typing.

'All right?' she asked.

'Dunno,' I said. 'I think I've cocked it up.'

She came over to me and looked through the papers.

'I need three Bs but I've got an A and a C and an F and I can't find one,' I cleared my throat. 'Sociology. That's it.'

'You've got a B,' she told me.

She has a sort of moustache growing over her top lip, but she's nice. Sometimes I think it must be good to have a mum like Mrs Price. I could smell her talcum powder.

'Go and have a word with Mr Harrington,' she told me. 'He'll sort you out.'

Tom could tell by my face that something was wrong but he just lowered his head and walked past me as if he didn't really know me. I hesitated outside Hippy Harrington's door. He can be such a pain, such a loud extrovert pain. I tried to put my face into a smile but my lips stuck together. He was whistling. When he saw me he jumped up, all energy and fuss. His arm swung across the top of his desk like the tail of a friendly dog, scattering his pile of papers.

'Good man, Chris!' he shouted. 'A for English! I knew you'd get there!'

He was so pleased that my lips peeled away from each other and I found myself grinning back at him. I actually began to think that I'd done it just for him, as a reward for all his enthusiasm and the kind of love he has for literature. None of the other teachers seemed to feel like that about their subjects. 'Language is power,' he used to say. 'Literature is love. And poetry is the food of the soul.' I'll always remember that, though I don't really know what he means. I remember once when we were doing a poetry appreciation class he read us a poem by Yeats and his hands were trembling when he opened the book. He read it out to us with such a reverence that it was as if he was giving us something very special, part of himself. Well, maybe I had got that A for him. It all seemed very remote now, all that reading, all that underlining in pencil and pacing round the house learning quotes. Just to please old Hippy.

'So, you're all set for Newcastle, eh, Chris?'

I told him about my results and he said he reckoned it would be fine, he'd ring up and see what he could do. 'You'll be fine, you'll be fine,' nodding at me like Father Christmas in a grotto.

I still stood there, feeling awkward. I didn't know what to say to him. Goodbye, or something like that. Thanks for everything. For Yeats, you know. I bent down to pick up his scattered papers and he bent down at the same time. From underneath his table he asked me, 'Where's your girlfriend off to, Chris? She's doing Music, isn't she? Manchester?' and I said, 'She's having a baby, Sir. We split.' He sank back on to his haunches, looking at me over the top of his desk, and I stood up slowly. I think I felt more awkward and wretched then than I've ever felt in my life.

'Poor kid,' he said. He must have meant Helen, or the baby. But the way he looked at me made my stomach turn over. It was as if he knew exactly how I felt.

There was nothing to say. I tipped the papers on to his desk and went home.

I rang Ruthlyn that evening. Her mother told me she was too upset to come to the phone. 'She got Bs all the way,' she told me. 'Bright as a diamond, that one, but it's not good enough, she says.'

'Poor old Ruthlyn,' I said. 'Does that mean she can't do Medicine?'

Coral blew down the receiver. I could imagine her big friendly face, worried and upset. 'She cryin' too much to tell me. It don't matter, I told her, you can help me with the kids. Cry cry cry!'

'You don't happen to know what Helen got, do you?'

'She's up with Ruthlyn now. She got all As.'

I stood there grinning down the receiver.

'Tell her I'm pleased,' I said. 'Tell Ruthlyn not to worry, she can resit them. And tell Helen I got A,B,C.'

I could hear Ruthlyn's mum scribbling away on a piece of paper, breathing through her teeth. 'A,B,C. You wanna tell her yourself? She's right here.'

'Yes, please!' The contents of my stomach suddenly sprinkled into minute droplets, all churning and shivering inside me. 'Helen,' I said. I could picture her tilting her head back, sweeping her hair away from her eyes the way she does, to let it swing loose again. I hadn't been able to picture her face properly for weeks. 'Helen?'

For a second I heard her voice again, whispering something to Coral.

'Now she's too upset to talk!' Coral's treacly voice came

back on the phone, sticky with sympathy. 'What can I do with these girls, Chris? You tell me and I'll do it.'

But I didn't answer her. I put the receiver down as slowly and carefully as if it was made of shell, as if any noise at all would shatter forever the brief, tiny, fragile sound I'd heard before Coral had spoken again; Helen's voice, after all these weeks. 'I can't.' I nursed the sound in my head, went up to my room and sat staring out into the evening, at trees billowing out in the wind and drizzle like fine net looping down. The cat pushed open the door and tiptoed over to me, didn't make a sound jumping on to my knee, lay there still and silent while Helen's soft voice formed and melted away again and again in my head, like drops of moisture at the fine point of an icicle.

A few days later my mother rang up. It was strange to hear her voice like that, bringing her suddenly into my consciousness. I imagined her room, with all those books in it, all those photographs lining the walls.

'I've got a few days free,' she said. I could tell she was smoking. 'I wonder if you'd like to come over and do a bit of climbing with me?'

I'd forgotten all about climbing. It felt as if it was somebody else, from years and years ago, who'd made those slippery and hopeless attempts on the climbing wall.

I couldn't even remember what it was I was trying to prove.

'I'm trying to sort out my university place,' I told her. 'Could I come next month?'

My dad was in the kitchen, moving dishes about quietly so as not to disturb me, half-listening, maybe. I wondered what he would say if my mother asked to speak to him.

'You can come whenever you want. Bring Helen, of course. How is she?'

'She's fine,' I said. Dad swung his head round at that.

'And what are your plans?'

My tongue was sticking in my throat. 'It's all a bit complicated at the moment.'

'Well. Tell me when you come up. Make it soon. We're looking forward to seeing you both again.'

'Fine, Mum. Joan. Thanks.'

Telephones are such alien things. They make fools and liars of us. How can you tell the truth when you're not looking people in the face? I felt lousy. How come I could tell my English teacher that Helen and I had split and not tell my mother? How come I could stand a few feet away from my dad and talk to my mother at the same time and try to pretend one of them didn't exist? Something was going on. Something was knitting up together like a cobweb in my head and had to be sorted out.

I went into the kitchen and stood watching Dad. He was making omelettes, cracking each egg separately into a bowl, sniffing them for freshness, tipping them out of their shells. The whites strung down in their clear, swaying strands, swinging the yolks down them like abseiling climbers. I watched for the moment when he punctured them, when the yellow juices sprawled out. And I don't know what it was that made me say this to him; I can only think it was something to do with the way he was lifting up the fork, just watching the spread of yolk, not trying to beat the eggs or anything. He was miles away. He wasn't thinking about omelettes or anything like that.

'Dad, did you mind Mum ringing me up?'

'Not particularly.' He still had his back to me, was still holding that elastic tension between fork and bowl as if he was being paid not to snap it.

'But you're all right, aren't you, the way things are?'

'Nearly,' he said. The egg strand snapped. 'Not quite.'

It was as if someone had opened a door and had slammed it shut again, and I'd just caught a glimpse of a secret room on the other side. Parents are such private people.

My next phone call came from Hippy, telling me there was no problem about my place at Newcastle.

'Great,' I said. My throat was as dry as a bone.

'Enjoy it,' he said. 'Make the most of it. Make the most of your life, Chris.'

It seemed as if you never had to make up your mind about things. They just happen, anyway, just tick into place.

Next morning I was lying in bed with a bit of a hangover when Guy put his head round the door to say there was someone outside for me.

'Tell him I'm dying,' I groaned.

'It's not a him.'

Guy disappeared and I shot out of bed. I crawled to the window on my hands and knees because I wasn't fit to be seen in public, but there was no sign of her. Guy's idea of a joke. I was about to collapse back into bed when I heard the sound of my dad's voice, and the light laugh of a girl. I rummaged round for clean socks, kicked the cat off my jeans and tee shirt in their last night's bundle and half-fell downstairs. My dad was standing in the hall and looking up at me with a quizzical expression that I couldn't fathom for the life of me, and then he stepped back and I saw who it was he was talking to. It was Bryn. She looked fantastic.

I sank back on to the stairs, pulling my socks on, pulling thoughts into my head.

'Hi, Slug!' she called up to me. 'What time d'you call this?'

'What are you doing here?' I asked.

'Come to see you, it looks like,' said Dad. He went into the kitchen. I could just tell that someone else was in there.

'I'm on my way to Leeds, looking for accommodation for next year. When the train stopped at Sheffield I couldn't believe it, so I decided to come and see you.'

'I don't believe it,' I said. I tried to stand up and sat down again. I could see Dad in the kitchen, shaking his head at someone, and realized that Jill was in there with a cup of coffee in her hand, staring at Bryn. Guy was messing about with his cagoule zip or something, standing between Bryn and the kitchen. I was sitting halfway up the stairs with one sock on and one sock off, peering through the banisters.

Bryn lost her smile, somehow. 'Aren't you pleased to see me?'

'Course I'm pleased to see you.'

Jill leaned forward and gently closed the kitchen door, and Guy looked up at me as if he'd been found guilty of eavesdropping and ran up the stairs, climbing over me.

I went down to Bryn. She looked very small and sunburnt.

'Hi,' I said. I couldn't think of anything else to say to her.

'I wouldn't mind a cup of coffee,' she said, shy suddenly. I couldn't face going into the kitchen with my dad and

Jill watching me, having to introduce her, explain where I'd met her and all that.

'We could have one at Tom's. I was just going round there, anyway.'

'Okay.'

He'd better be in, I thought. I couldn't imagine where else I'd take her. I ran back upstairs for my shoes. My nerves were bubbling up. I couldn't find my comb. I could have done with a shave. I could have done with a wash, actually, but the sooner we could get out of the house the better. I ran downstairs to her and then had to run upstairs again for my key. I felt as if we had a train to catch. As we went out I saw her little rucksack in the hall and told her to bring it with her. She looked disappointed. I felt lousy, lousy.

It was raining by the time we got to the end of the street.

'I suppose we'd better go back,' I said, soaked. I had nothing on over my tee shirt.

'Not at all,' she said, in a tight, high voice. 'I have to be in Leeds by this afternoon.'

'That's a shame,' I said.

'And I'd like to see Tom.'

'Oh, so would he. Like to see you, I mean.'

We were as polite to each other as strangers on railway trains. I couldn't shake it off. I couldn't believe that less than a month ago we'd been lounging round in French campsites, messing about as if we'd known each other for years. My head was thick with thoughts of that riverbank, the crickets chirring, that insect drone. Maybe, like wine, sun goes straight to my head.

'How did your results go?' she asked.

I pulled a face. 'I've scraped in on points. Dropped a couple of grades.'

'So did I,' she grinned. 'All the results were terrible at our school. We're asking for re-marks.'

'But you're in.'

'Yes, I'm in. That's the main thing.'

The rain was running like worms down my neck, and my hair was flat over my eyes. I was a bit worried about the design on my tee shirt. I'd done it myself, and it hadn't been washed yet. I'd feel a right idiot if it started running. But really, that was the least of my problems.

'What's up?'

'Nothing's up. It's the surprise, that's all. I didn't expect you.'

'Okay,' she said. 'So you don't like surprises. That's fair enough.'

We walked on in silence. I used to think Tom's house was near mine. It seemed miles away. Anyway, luckily he was in. He made everything all right, old Tom.

'I can't believe it,' he kept laughing. 'You in Sheffield, Bryn!'

He brought out his photographs of France and spread them out on the carpet, and Bryn brought hers out of her rucksack. We were soon rolling about laughing at them, and remembering things about people we'd met on the campsites – Monsieur Bienvenu and all the other characters – Jeremy Stereotype with all his family of typelets, the Fish at the End of the Universe, Bassoon-voice. We kept remembering things and spluttering them out at each other. It was nerves. I was in a state of advanced hysteria.

Tom suggested we should walk Bryn down to the station and pick up some chips on the way. The sun was out again when we set off. We were still in a daft mood; and fate did the rest. I just don't think it could have happened if we hadn't had that mad spell in Tom's house. I bent down to tie my laces and for some inane reason Tom just hoicked Bryn into the air and lowered her on to my shoulders. She yelled out and clung to my hair with both hands, and I stood up very slowly with my back straight so she wouldn't tip off. We were all yelling with laughter. I couldn't see a thing because she'd pushed her hands over my eyes, but I started to walk forward, holding out my arms to balance myself, like a circus act. Then Tom stopped laughing and put his hand on my arm.

I pushed Bryn's hands out of my eyes and held them out to the sides, our fingers locking so she could hold on tight. And then I saw what Tom had seen, and wished I hadn't. Two girls had stopped at the end of the road and were just turning away. It was like seeing another door swinging open and slamming shut again, only this time there was no secret room on the other side of it. One of the girls was black. The other was small and fair. I hardly recognized her, she'd changed so much.

★ ★ ★

Dear Nobody,

I hate him! I hate him! I hate him!

September

Dear Nobody,

I can't believe it's only about two weeks to go. Deep, deep inside me there's that screaming still, that fear; and at the same time there's a kind of calm. I can't wait to know you. I wish you could just magically appear. Well, we have got a gooseberry bush in the garden. I'm afraid of the pain, Nobody. I can't help being afraid of it. I hope we like each other. I mean, really like. I wonder what my mum thought when she first saw me.

My father has bought a cot for you. It was a most extraordinary thing, seeing him struggling in from the car with it, realizing what it was, looking at Mum straight away to catch the expression on her face, and seeing nothing there. She wants you to be adopted, still. She just pursed her lips then and followed him upstairs, and I heard them banging about, moving my bed to make room for it. I followed them up.

'I'm staying here, then?' I said.

'Of course she's staying here,' my father said to Mum.

'Where else would you go, tell me that?' she demanded. 'This arrangement won't do forever, just remember that. And don't leave that thing up,' she said to him. 'Not till it's born.'

She went into her own room and closed the door. I wanted to follow her but Dad shook his head at me.

'She has her own way of coping, Helen. Leave her,' he said. After all, it seems he understands her.

I sank down on to my bed. The sides of the cot were propped against the wall. It was pale lemon, with rabbits in little blue and pink rompers prancing along the bars. 'How can I stay here if I'm not wanted?'

Dad cleared his throat and squatted down in front of me, his long bony fingers resting flat along his thighs. 'Of course you're wanted. Get that out of your head. You're our daughter. Never forget that. It wasn't in our scheme of things to have a baby living in the house . . .'

'It wasn't in my scheme of things, either.'

'We don't want to lose you, you know.'

I shook my head and he lifted up one of his hands and just touched my cheek; a shy, unfamiliar gesture.

'You're to stay here as long as you want to. That's my promise. And your promise to me, Helen, is that you won't let your music go. One day you'll dance again. Promise me that.'

I did promise him, though the screaming in my head was loud enough to drown us all. Maybe it was you, making your whale noises deep inside me. For a long time after he'd gone out of the room and into their bedroom I sat there, listening to that screaming, counting the rabbits in their never-ending joyous prancing round and round the sides of the cot, flopsy-bunnying for all the babies in the world. I could hear Mum and Dad in their room, consoling each other in whatever way it is that married people do. I wondered if he was loving her.

I went out then, to see my nan and Grandad. I can't remember when I last went there with my mother, I was thinking, or whether my nan had ever been to our house to see us there. I wondered whether that wound would ever heal, whether there ever came a time in people's sorrowings when forgiveness was easier than pain. But what I did know was that I wouldn't live with Nan now. How could I bear her silences? One day I want to try to creep inside her mind and talk to her; after all, we have a lot in common. I want to ask her about my real grandad, the dancer in a nightclub. I'm holding that in my head, a tiny warm promise, for the right moment. I wonder why it's so hard for young people to talk to old people about the things that really matter. But then, it's hard to talk to Nan about anything at all.

Her eyes lit up when I went in to her room that day, just a brief blaze of light, and then faded away to daydreaming again. I know about you, Nan. I have your secret in my head. I went over to her and put my arms round her. She had a lovely, soapy smell.

'I've got a present for you,' she told me.

It was a shawl for you. Grandad told me he'd had to bring all the boxes down from the attic, and that she'd spent hours rummaging through the past to find it. It must have been my mum's when she was a baby. Perhaps it was her own, the child in the drawer. She spread it out for me to touch. Then, instead of giving it to me, she just sat there with the thing rolled up on her knee, staring down at it.

'It's lovely, Nan,' I said. She was slipping away again. I touched her dry and papery hand.

'She probably wants to wash it before she gives it to you,' Grandad said. 'It's years old.'

She looked at him, then, as if he'd just walked off a space ship. 'How can I give it her before the baby's born?' she asked him. 'It might be dead!'

Oh little thing, be alive! Be well. Be perfect for me.

No, how could we live at Nan's? I want you to be able to yell your head off when you feel like it, and not annoy people. I want us both to be able to yell our heads off.

★ ★ ★

September 21st

My dear Helen,

I know you are an independent young woman who will make up her own mind about things. I admire you for it. Whatever plans you make for your future, I wish you well with them. You are a survivor, whatever happens. You have that quality in you. You and your baby will need money, and I would like to make a contribution till Chris is able to do it for himself, though I don't want him or his father to know about this. There will be a sum paid monthly into an account for your child, and I hope you will accept it. I also hope, Helen, that one day you will be willing to let me meet my grandchild.

Joan

★ ★ ★

She has terrible handwriting. It's like unravelling a tangle of inky knitting. I can't take it in, the words of her letter, but it made me cry all the same, as if someone had put a blanket of comfort round me in the night.

All I can focus on is you, thrusting and pushing inside me all these weeks, turning yourself round. You've settled yourself now for coming out, the midwife told me yesterday. You've got a long and dark and frightening journey ahead of you soon. Don't be afraid. We'll manage it together.

* * *

It was the middle of September before I got round to buying the books on the reading list they'd sent me from Newcastle. I enjoyed browsing round the students' second-hand bookshops, though, picking up tatty copies of leather-bound volumes of Milton and Shelley and poets like that, just names to me, that had passed from hand to hand. The pages inside were all scored with underlinings and pencil notes, all in different writing, and I suddenly felt excited at the thought of joining in the long line of scholars from other centuries, other ages. I imagined monks in gloomy cells, bowed over their manuscripts, the scratching of quills on parchment. I bought a little red-leather copy of an ancient poem called *Beowulf*. It was written in Anglo-Saxon. I couldn't understand a word of it.

It was the most amazing thing in the world to walk into my house that afternoon and see my mother there. I didn't know what on earth to say to her. I opened the door and was just about to go upstairs to my room when I heard her voice in the kitchen. My stomach went cold inside me. Maybe it was shock. I ran upstairs and tried to sort out my head before I faced her. I could hear her down in the kitchen below, laughing out loud. I couldn't understand it; I couldn't understand why she was here, or why I felt so shaken up at the thought of seeing her here, in our house. I couldn't work out in my head what the hell to say to her. Maybe, I thought, just maybe, she was planning to come back here to live with us. Did I want that? No, I didn't want that now. I felt sad inside, frustrated and angry and sad, screwed up so tight that it hurt. It was too late. When I was a little boy of ten I desperately wanted my mother back home, and if you'd asked me why I'd have said it was because she'd have made sure my sports stuff was clean and ready for Wednesdays, and I wouldn't have had to go to Cubs in the rain, and I wouldn't be shouted at for having nosebleeds. Perhaps I'd have said that Dad wouldn't have sat for hours with his head in his hands, night after night. Guy wouldn't have had to cry himself to sleep. It was too late now. Nothing would ever put that right.

I couldn't understand myself. I wanted to write letters to

my mother and to talk to her on the phone, and to drop in and see her when it suited me. I didn't want to see her chopping up onions in our kitchen, sitting with her feet up on our settee watching television, coming out of Dad's room in his dressing gown.

I had a wash and put on a decent sweatshirt and went downstairs. I could hear the babble of voices surging up in a confused kind of frenzy of laughing and talking, and as soon as I went into the kitchen it stopped. It was as if I'd pushed it behind the door as I opened it. There was my mother, looking terrific. That bloke of hers was there. Dad was there, his voice tailing off last of all, in the middle of some yarn about Guy and his telescope. I stared round at them all. Jill was standing next to Dad. I'd forgotten that she and my mother are sisters. And Guy was perched on the stool blinking at the cat.

'Hi,' I said. I felt awkward, like a six-year-old who's burst in on a grown-up party.

Don shoved a glass of frothy bubbles at me. I guessed it must be champagne. Horrible stuff. They all stared at me, and I held it up and took a sip. 'Here's to . . .' I said. Anything to fill that silence.

'Our divorce,' my mother said.

'I don't get it,' I said.

'You do get it,' said Guy, earnest little owl, bright-eyed and pale as death.

But I didn't. I didn't understand why words like that would make them all smile at me, coaxing me to smile back, and I was the spoilsport at the party, the drab in the corner who never gets a joke, the wet blanket, whatever that's supposed to mean. I didn't want to play games. I didn't know the rules.

'Your father and I are getting a divorce,' said my mother.

'Well, that's wonderful,' I said, dry. 'And I thought you did that years ago.'

'Our marriage. Drink to it, Christopher.' Don held out his hand to me. I thought of making some daft remark about not fancying him enough to marry him, but I couldn't be bothered. No one would have got it, anyway. 'I thought you were already married,' I said, ignoring his hand. 'Or were you just practising?'

They all roared with laughter as if I was the clown that they'd all been waiting for.

'It means,' said my mother, 'that Don and I have thought long and carefully about marriage, and what it involves. And we know that we're ready to take that step.'

I looked at Dad. 'And I know they're right for each other,' he said. I understood then. He was letting her go.

I raised my glass and drained it down. I swallowed back a burp. I felt very drunk, but not in that giggly, smiling give-us-a-cuddle way of theirs. I shook hands with all of them, even Guy, and then I stepped past all their legs and out into the back yard and threw my glass against the wall.

It was beautiful, the way that perfect shell burst apart and splintered; the way the stars of glass caught light and soared before they fell.

It's strange how you can go for years and years letting other people be responsible for the way you think and dress and eat, what you learn, how you speak, and all of a sudden you find you've broken away from all that web of protection and you're free.

Over the next few days I got to know my mother and Don quite well. They stayed in a hotel in Derbyshire and I cycled over there a few times and then went for walks with them. I was surprised to find that I liked him.

'Come on, Christopher, take us to your favourite places,' he said. I enjoyed doing that. I didn't take them anywhere near the Edge where I'd tried to climb that time, or any of my special Helen places. I only ever go there on my own. But I did take them to the top of Burbage, and we sat on a big rock under the bridge so we could look right down the valley, all the colours turning, and the sheeps' backs muzzy with September light, and I said, 'This is where my childhood is, Mum.' I didn't care whether it sounded corny or not.

I'm glad I had those few days with her. I liked her a lot. And I wanted to call her Mum, not Joan, I found. So I did. Names are weird things.

But when she asked me about my future plans I clammed up. My future had been decided for me.

'I haven't spoken to Helen since the end of June,' I said.

'I gathered that,' Mum said. 'But can you put it all behind you?'

'Like hell I can.'

Maybe I won't go to Newcastle, I told her. Maybe I'll go on the road, pack up my rucksack and freewheel round the world. How far away from Helen could I get and not think about her? If it takes light less than a second to circle the planet, would she see me from the other side? How long does sound take? If I stood by Ayres Rock and whispered 'Nell', would she hear it in her dreamings? If there was nothing else in the way, no engines or machinery or laughter or shouting or crying, maybe she'd hear it. Europe, Africa, India, Japan, Australia. If I cycled for ever and ever, shouting her name, would that help?

'It takes time,' Mum said.

A few days after Don and Mum went back up north I had a letter from Bryn. It was full of jokes and funny drawings and bits of poems. It went on for pages. She finished up by asking me to come and see her one day when she was in Leeds. 'I miss you,' she said. It hurt to read it. I knew for sure what I'd been guessing when we were in France together, and from the way she'd looked at me when she came to my house that day. I remember the way she'd been after we'd seen Ruthlyn and Helen in the street. I remember now how I stooped down to let her climb off my back, and then I'd just stuck my hands in my pockets and headed back for home, with my head cracking like a machine gun. She and Tom had come after me and walked with me; Bryn had had to run to keep up with me, I remember that, and I'd tried to shake her off the way you shake off a wasp that's bothering you. But it wasn't her fault. I'd turned round to tell her that and she'd just stood there, with her face, smiling and puzzled and sorry, turned up to mine, and for some reason that I don't understand I'd just bent down and kissed her, a friend's kiss, a please-don't-blame-yourself kiss. So we'd gone on to buy chips and then to see her off at the station, and I could tell by the way she smiled goodbye to me that she did blame herself, and what's more, that as far as she was concerned we were far more than just friends. I hadn't written to her though, and I hadn't heard from her. I'd thought, that's it. It's over now.

And then her letter came, bubbling with Bryn. I could hear her voice and her laugh in every word I read. I knew it would never work the way she wanted it. There was too much of me that was hurt, tied up in something that I couldn't work out, never would work out, like the threads of a spider's web that won't ever snap.

So I did this: I wrote her a letter to say that I liked her very much but that I didn't think we should ever meet again. I knew it would hurt her, and I didn't feel any better for writing it. I felt bad. But I had to do it, so I did.

★ ★ ★

September 30th

Dear Nobody,

I feel peculiar tonight. Terrible. I can hardly walk in fact. You've moved right down. Dropped, the midwife said. Turned, ready for action. I wish I was. I feel more like going to sleep, for a long, long time. You'll be here in a few days, if you're punctual.

I'm gross. I'm a tub of butter. I don't know myself these days. Once upon a time there was a girl called Helen who could dance. She could actually bend in the middle. What middle? Then she turned into a fat caterpillar and then she became a pupa and went into a state of coma. And a fairy godmother called a midwife came to see her and said, 'Cinderhelen, you WILL go to the hospital. You will emerge

224

out of your chrysalis.' But the amazing thing is, there won't just be one butterfly emerging, shaking trembly wings. There'll be two, you and me. And the sad thing is, there won't be a handsome prince. There won't be any prince at all.

I wish it was all over.

God, I'm so fed up.

★ ★ ★

The day before I was due to set off for Newcastle I bought some new jeans. They felt really peculiar because they hadn't got holes in the knees. Mum had given me some money to buy a quilt cover, of all things, but I didn't bother to get that. But I did window shop a bit, looking at some pale blue, floaty material that reminded me of the dress Helen wore at that last dance we were at. There was a bit of poetry that kept coming into my head. 'He Wishes for the Cloths of Heaven', it's called. It was one of the ones Hippy Harrington read to us, gave us I suppose, by that Irish poet, Yeats. I know it off by heart. He's right, Hippy. You should learn poetry by heart; then you own it, in a strange kind of way.

> Had I the heavens' embroidered cloths,
> Enwrought with golden and silver light,
> The blue and the dim and the dark cloths

Of night and light and the half-light,
I would spread the cloths under your feet:
But I, being poor, have only my dreams;
I have spread my dreams under your feet;
Tread softly because you tread on my dreams.

I bought a postcard and wrote it down. No need to sign it. I walked down her road after that, with those words banging away in my head like music. I just thought I might see her and be able to say goodbye to her in a natural way. There's no way I'm going to phone up again and suffer the humiliation of having the receiver put down on me. They've built a protective wall around Helen that's too high to climb over and too thick to break through, and too deeply founded to tunnel under, and it's something to do with the fact that they love her. I understand all that now; but it's a funny kind of love. I walked past the house, looking and not looking at it. It was as neat as ever. They've got money, that family. Funny. I hadn't even thought about that before.

I hate this silence. It's like a bandage, wrapped round my mouth and my ears. Speak to me.

I found myself in the library where Helen's father works. He grinned away when he saw me and came tiptoeing over with his hands behind his back.

'How's the guitar coming on?'

I knew he'd say that.

'Fine,' I said. I looked out of the window and then back at him before he moved away. 'How's Helen, Mr Garton?'

He looked a little confused. Nice bloke, Mr Garton. Wouldn't want to hurt anyone's feelings, you can tell that. His brain was working out that this was a taboo subject and that he was standing there with no defences.

'She's looking very large,' he said. 'Like a potato.'

I swallowed hard.

'I'm going away the day after tomorrow, Mr Garton. Will you . . . will you give her this.' I handed him the card.

You'd think I'd pulled a live snake out of my pocket and put it into his hands, and that he didn't know what to do with it, whether to stamp on it or shove it in his pockets out of sight or hold it out and admire it for the rare thing that it was. Anyway, I left him with it. I didn't shake hands with him, as I would have done, as he'd have liked, probably. It would have made him feel better. But he's old enough to handle snakes, I think.

* * *

September 30th

Yesterday I cleaned my room out, ready for you.

I took all my books off the shelves and the glass and

porcelain animals I've collected since I was little, the pottery masks and fans on my walls, and I washed and dusted them all. I washed all my floating scarves. I even took the curtains down and washed them and put them out on the line to dry. Mum helped me to peg them out, and I stood watching them after she'd gone back into the kitchen. They were like birds' wings, flapping for freedom. I felt as if I was rising up, rising up with them. I went back into the kitchen and sat with Mum having lunch; we were both sitting by the window, staring out at these huge flapping wings, saying nothing. But we weren't apart, you know, Mum and I. We weren't locking each other out.

September 30th

A few minutes ago, I felt a massive kind of cramp rising up from the base of my spine, right up, spreading out and up till it held me in the centre of it. It seemed to take hold of my whole body and when I felt I was going to burst with it it died away again.

I'm not frightened. I know exactly what it is.

It means you're coming.

I've made my bed. I've put my case ready by the door.

I'm not going to tell Mum until I have another contraction. It could go on for hours or days even, the midwife told me. I want us both to be ready for this, you and me. I want us to be calm and ready.

Breathe slowly, both of us. I feel as if I can hear your heart beating, deep in my veins.

Here it comes. Again. Rising and rising. It's a huge soaring white wave and I'm going under in it. Don't let me drown. Hold on. Don't let me drown.

I know you're coming.

I didn't know I was doing it but I've been screaming out, 'Mum! Mum!' She ran into my room and I tried to walk over to her. I felt something pouring out of me. She put her arms round me and held me through the next one. We rose up on it together. I felt as if I was being born. I cried out loud, and she held me tight and took the pain for me.

She's phoning for the ambulance now, downstairs. I can't stop shaking.

Dad was playing the piano. That's his way of coping with it. Did you hear it? It's a song of welcome. But then I heard Mum shouting at him and he stopped playing. He came up to my room and stood in the doorway. I was propped up on the bed, waiting for the midwife to come, or the ambulance, whichever turns up first. I started trembling again when I saw Dad. He came over to me and took something from his pocket.

'I think you should have this now,' he said. 'It's from Chris.'

When he went back down, back to his piano, I read it. I took it to the window and stood there looking at it in the light of the street lamp. I could hear Chris's voice, that slight hesitation he has, reading the words to me. I turned round, aware of a sound behind me, to see Robbie in the doorway, looking important and shy and a bit scared. He crept in as if I was dying.

'I've come to see if I can do anything to help,' he said.

If I hadn't been hurting so much I would have smiled. But then I realized that he *could* help.

'Robbie,' I said. 'Will you take something to Chris for me?'

So he's gone down to get his bike out of the shed, my Mercury, while I make up the parcel. Dear Nobody. This is the last letter I'll write to you.

★ ★ ★

October

I took the package up to my room and opened it there. It was just a pile of letters. They all began the same way.

Dear Nobody.

Is that what I'd become to her, then?

I sat down on the bed with a growing kind of grief inside me, and began to read them in order. They took me back to January.

When I finished reading them I felt as if I was hung in space. There was no air around me, only blackness, cold and empty and vast. I lumbered downstairs. Dad and Jill were sitting watching a late film on television. There was my rucksack, packed and ready for Newcastle, propped up against the wall. It was almost midnight.

'The baby's coming,' I told them, and left them there with their faces open and gasping like fishes. I walked out into the yard. The air slapped me back to life.

I hauled my bike out of the shed, clattering over the stepladder and a sack of potatoes and tins of paint. I didn't care how much row I made. I set off straight for the hospital, so focused that it was as if a magnet was drawing me there. I don't think I've ever ridden so fast in my life. I threw the bike into a bush and ran into the foyer.

'Where's Helen?' I asked the woman at the reception desk. For the life of me I couldn't remember her surname. At last it popped up and I was told the ward number. I ran off through a labyrinth of corridors that seemed to be a freeway for trolleys and stretchers. I came to a little side ward, stopped and leaned against the corridor wall, dredging up air from somewhere. Let her be all right. Oh, let her be all right.

I pushed the door open. Helen's parents were there, standing round the bed. When I burst in they turned round to stare at me. The room started swinging round like the pendulum of a clock. My legs were too heavy to move. My breath was corked up in my throat.

Mr Garton moved back and somehow I got myself to the bed. Helen was smiling. She was pale and tired and smiling.

'Chris,' she said. 'Look.'

I saw something that was tiny and red-faced, crinkled-up, sleeping, breathing, an unbelievable still presence in the room.

So, in my student's room in Newcastle, I'm writing this for you, Amy. Your name means loved one, or friend, and we both chose it. This is your story, and you should know it. One day a long time from now you will read it and put together all the bits and pieces of people that have gone together to make you.

One day I hope to really know you. I only know the beginning of your story.

When I saw you that day at the hospital I realized that during all those months of separation from Helen I hadn't thought once about you. You were nobody. It was Helen I was thinking about day and night, night and day. I wanted to be with her and to hold her. I wanted everything to be the same again. But when I saw her at last, you were there. I was shocked by your importance, by your vulnerability. The thought of holding you or even touching you scared me, tiny creature that you were. I tried to look at you and say, she is ours, and I couldn't. I felt weak. I wanted to hide from you.

Helen is right. I'm not ready for you, or for her. I'm not yet ready for myself.

November

Dear Chris,

I think I'm exactly where I want to be, at this moment of my life. I think of you often, with love, and I hope you're happy, too.

Today my nan came to the house. It wasn't easy for her to come, I know that. We sat in the front room together; Nan on the hard chair, Mum by the window, me in the low nursing chair with Amy. Nan didn't say much, but then, you wouldn't expect her to. She just watched me, in that sad, nodding way of hers. When I finished feeding Amy and was just about to put her down, all milky-sweet and sleepy, Mum came over and took her from me. She just kissed her, the way she does, and then she walked back across the room and put her in Nan's arms.

It was as though Amy was a fine thread being drawn through a garment, mending tears.

THE ORIGINALS
Iconic • Outspoken • First

💡 FOR THINKERS

- ☐ **Dear Nobody**
  Berlie Doherty

- ☐ **Buddy**
  Nigel Hinton

- ☐ **The Red Pony**
  John Steinbeck

- ☐ **The Wave**
  Morton Rhue

♡ FOR LOVERS

- ☐ **I Capture the Castle**
  Dodie Smith

- ☐ **Across the Barricades**
  Joan Lingard

- ☐ **The Twelfth Day of July**
  Joan Lingard

- ☐ **Postcards from No Man's Land**
  Aidan Chambers

✊ FOR REBELS

- ☐ **The Outsiders**
  S. E. Hinton

- ☐ **The Pearl**
  John Steinbeck

- ☐ **No Turning Back**
  Beverley Naidoo

☢ FOR SURVIVORS

- ☐ **Z for Zachariah**
  Richard C. O'Brien

- ☐ **After the First Death**
  Robert Cormier

- ☐ **Stone Cold**
  Robert Swindells

- ☐ **The Endless Steppe**
  Esther Hautzig

What are you reading? Tell **@penguinplatform #OriginalYA**

YouTube

LOVE AGAINST THE ODDS . . .

THE ORIGINALS

. . . in genteel poverty

. . . in Belfast during the Troubles

. . . across a religious divide

. . . in occupied England

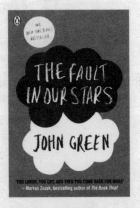

. . . in a cancer support group

. . . in a segregated society

What's your story?   **#OriginalYA**